ABOUT SNOWBOUND SQUEEZE

A SPECIAL PONDEROSA RESORT NOVELLA!

Rule one when seeking a secret mountain hideaway: Be certain the cabin's unoccupied. Also, make sure there's no blizzard coming.

I've screwed up all of that before I get the key in the door, which shouldn't be a shock. God knows I've messed up plenty of things lately. Is it too much to want a hideout from Hollywood headlines in a place no one knows my name?

Maybe not, since Gretchen Laslo has zero clue who I am. That's the upside of being snowed-in with a stunning professor whose impressive list of appliances includes two ice cream makers and no television.

The downside? Cocoa and blanket forts lead to toe-curling sex, which leads to me kinda-sorta forgetting to tell her the paparazzi's on my tail.

It's a matter of time before she finds out. When that happens, our wintry romance will melt faster than a pair of snowmen boning in a sauna.

8

TAWNA FENSKE

Trapped
in
paradise

Snowbound
SQUEEZE

A Ponderosa Resort Romantic Comedy

SNOWBOUND SQUEEZE

A PONDEROSA RESORT NOVELLA

TAWNA FENSKE

Dedicated to my street team, Fenske's Frisky Posse. Thank you for naming my characters, dressing me for events, and generally keeping me sane. You're the best batch of unpaid cheerleaders any author could ask for, and I can't imagine doing this without you.

- Just for Show (Cooper & Amy coming soon!)
- Show and Tell (Lana & Dal coming soon!)
- Show of Hands (Tia & Vonn coming soon!)

CHAPTER 1

GABLE

I don't know if I've ever been this tired. Bone deep, balls dragging the floor exhausted.

As I sag against my buddy's front door, he drops the key into my palm. I curl my fist around the metal lifeline and hold tight.

"Stay as long as you need to." James's voice is pitched low, and I hate the pity in his eyes.

Pity and whatever it's called when a dude has three sparkly red lipstick marks on his face.

"Thank you." I force the words past the tightness in my throat and try not to stare at the kiss print just above his jaw. Did Lily miss his mouth on purpose? "And—uh—no one else knows about this? Me being in Oregon."

James braces an arm against the cedar-planked wall of his cabin's foyer. He has questions, and I'm grateful he's not asking them. Grateful we're doing this here. That he's not luring me in for wine and friendly catch-up.

I'm not feeling friendly. Just tired. Tired and really fucking raw.

Also confused about the lipstick. Seriously, does he not know it's there?

"Lily knows," James says, and it takes me a second to remember what we're talking about. "I told her you were headed this way. She's been worried since we saw everything on the news."

"I'm fine." I don't know if I'm trying to convince him or me.

"The rest of resort management doesn't know you're here," he assures me. "And they definitely don't know about that."

He nods at the key, and I clutch it tighter. "Thanks."

I've met most of James's siblings and love the crap out of them, but right now, I need discretion. "Privacy's sort of key at the moment."

"You'll have that in spades at the cabin," he says. "To be honest, I think everyone forgot it exists. We inherited it together, but it's so far in the middle of nowhere that no one ever uses it."

Perfect.

James rubs a hand over his chin, narrowly missing a smear of lipstick. I debate mentioning it but decide not to. I won't be here long, and there's no sense embarrassing him. I'm sure he's eager to get back to whatever produced the lip prints in the first place.

A gust of wind hurls ice chips at the door behind me, and I glance out the window to my left. Trees sway in the darkness, their needles flickering with moonlight.

"The snow's not supposed to hit until tomorrow night," James says. "You should be fine."

"I will be."

I'm not sure we're talking about snow.

He studies my face for a moment. "I wasn't sure you were still coming."

"It took me a while to get out of town. LA traffic, you know?"

He nods, making the lipstick on his left temple flash in the light from the sconce beside the door. "Right. Still, I was worried."

James isn't the only one. It's my agent who finally persuaded me to get out of town. "Perhaps you should find someplace to lay low," he suggested on the phone last week. "Just stay out of the public eye until things quiet down."

My brother, Dean, was more direct. "Get the fuck out of Hollywood," he growled. "Hide out until we tell you to come back. Or fuck it, don't come back. God knows I'd love to get out of here."

So that's what I'm doing. Getting lost, at least for a little while.

The key feels warm in my palm, its metal ridges biting into the fleshy undersides of my fingers. I should get going.

"Thanks again," I say, taking a step back. "I'll get out of your—"

"Gable!" James's fiancée swoops in wearing a silky red kimono belted at the waist. Lily pulls me into a soft, fragrant hug, reminding me again that my college pal is one lucky son of a bitch. "We weren't sure you'd make it. How's your family?"

"Great." I channel as much enthusiasm as possible into that syllable, adding a smile for good measure. "Lana and Lauren and Mari say hi. They keep asking when you're coming back to visit."

"We're hoping they'll come see us this time." She smiles and glances at James. I see her register the lipstick on his face the same instant he pushes off the wall and launches into full-on CEO mode.

"I really think you'd be better off staying here." He's pacing like a courtroom lawyer, which he was once upon a time. "We've got a full-time security team at Ponderosa Resort."

Lily nods, choosing to ignore the lipstick in favor of ganging up on me. "He's right. The resort's full for Valentine's weekend, so we'd have lots of eyes and ears watching out for you."

This sounds as appealing as smashing my testicles in the cutlery drawer. "I appreciate the offer, but I'm really looking for some alone time."

The two exchange a look I can't read. That's possibly because the red smear beside James's mouth makes his polished façade look vaguely clownlike.

Lily lifts a hand to wipe it at the same moment James turns and sweeps a hand toward their living room. "We have a guest suite that's very private," he insists. "You could have meals brought in and would never have to interact with anyone."

Dropping her hand, Lily gives an infinitesimal shrug and regards me with a bemused smile. "We're very discreet."

The kindness in her eyes is almost enough to change my mind.

Almost. "This cabin will be perfect." I shove the key in my pocket before they can snatch it back. "No phones, no internet, no television."

No calls from my agent, no hate mail, no televised reminders of my great fuckup.

James sighs and yanks at his tie. Tries to anyway, but there isn't one. Whatever they were doing when I got here jettisoned his ever-present neckwear.

Lily sticks her hands in the pockets of her kimono and regards me with concern. "We sent someone out to the cabin to get it ready for you," she says. "It's clean, but it's really rustic. You know how to chop firewood and all that?"

"I've got some dynamite left over from that last action flick," I deadpan. "Figure I can use it to fell a couple trees."

Lily laughs, then whips a tissue out of her pocket and raises it in triumph. She edges toward James, poised to swipe.

And misses, because now he's pacing again. "Look, we're just worried about you." He rakes his fingers through his hair, smearing the lip print at his right temple. "Maybe if you talk to someone about—"

"I'm fine," I insist, more urgently this time. "Really, I promise. I just need to go somewhere no one recognizes me and no one's reminding me of what happened."

There's that look again, that silent exchange between two

people who know each other well enough to have a full conversation with no words. I'd envy them if I weren't a jaded asshole intent on being alone.

Lily looks back at me and sighs. "At least promise you'll be careful. And that you'll go into town at least once to call and let us know you're okay."

"Promise." I put a hand on my heart the way James and I used to do when reciting the school pledge, and my heart twists at the memory. How did life get so messed up?

"Fine," James says. "Can we at least feed you dinner?"

"Not hungry." My stomach chooses that moment to rumble like a gravel crusher.

Lily arches one eyebrow. "Really?"

I reach behind me for the doorknob, determined to flee before they tie me to a dining room chair and force coq au vin down my throat. I wrench the door open, walking backwards in case they try to tackle me. "Fine, I'm starving. I haven't eaten since I left LA. I promise I'll eat on the way. I just want to get—"

"Whoa! Heads up, big guy."

The female voice registers half a second before I crash into the female body. The very soft, very warm female body.

I whirl around, stumbling as I turn to face—

"Holy shit." The words slip out before I consider this is not the way to greet a total stranger.

But this stranger is the most stunning woman I've ever seen. Hair the color of warm caramel is piled on her head in a swoopy, loopy bun. Eyes like blue sea glass spark with light from the porch, and there's a dusting of cinnamon freckles on her nose. She's wearing—clothes, I think. I can't look away from her face to check out the rest of her.

She laughs and flips a stray lock of hair off her face. "Okay, not the greeting I'm used to, but hello." Her smile is warm, and there's not a trace of makeup on her face. "Gretchen." She extends her hand to me. "Sorry to startle you. I just came over to borrow dill."

"Dill." I pat my pockets absurdly like I might have some tucked away. "I—um—"

"I'll get it." Lily hustles away. "What are you making?" she calls from the kitchen.

"My famous salmon chowder." Gretchen gives me that smile again, and my guts turn to chowder. "It's a family recipe."

I'm too dumbstruck to think of a response, so James comes to my rescue. "Gretchen is my brother Jonathan's sister."

"Your sister," I repeat, only catching some of his words. Seriously, I had no idea sweatpants could be so sexy. How have I never met this woman?

"Not *his* sister." Gretchen shoves her hands in the pockets of her blue hoodie, which matches her eyes almost perfectly. "The Bracelyn family tree is kind of a mess. Jon's the second oldest, but we have different dads. I'm not a Bracelyn at all."

Lily rushes back to us with a glass jar and presses it into Gretchen's hand. "Gretchen's been staying out here while she's at OSU Cascades. She's an adjunct professor and an absolutely brilliant researcher."

"A researcher." I look back at her, watching as her eyes scan my face. I brace for the flicker of recognition in her eyes. For what comes next. What *always* comes next.

Wait. Didn't I see you in an article about—

Aren't you the guy who—

Don't I know you from—

"Want some soup?"

I blink as Gretchen holds up the glass jar of dill. "This is the finishing touch. I made a ton of it and I heard you say you were starving."

I did say that.

But I also said I was leaving. Hitting the road, getting far, far away from here as soon as possible. I should definitely do that.

"I'd love some soup."

What the hell?

"Great." Gretchen grins. "I'm sorry, I didn't catch your name. And I'm hoping you're a friend of James and Lily and that I didn't just invite the vacuum cleaner salesman to dinner."

"Gabl—Gabe," I stammer.

God, that was dumb. Even with the abbreviated version of my name, she's going to recognize me. Put two and two together and figure it out.

Weren't you the one who—

"Gabe and I are friends from school," James supplies. "And Gretchen—reads a lot."

I'm trying to figure out what that has to do with anything when she laughs again. "That's his polite way of saying I don't get out much. Probably why I'm accosting strangers with dinner invitations. It's okay, you don't have to come in and sit there making awkward dinner conversation if you don't want. I can package up the chowder for you to take wherever you were going."

Where was I going?

Right. The cabin. The remote cabin in the woods more than an hour from here. I should be getting on the road.

"I'm not in a hurry," I hear myself saying. "I'd love to join you."

"Great." She quirks an eyebrow at James and Lily. "You'd tell me if he was a serial killer, right?"

My gut twists at her words. I'm grateful she's not looking at me. That she missed the wince, the flash of guilt I'm positive flickered in my eyes just now.

But James catches it. He's staring at me, icy gaze boring hard into mine. "Not a serial killer." He speaks the words to me, like he's willing me to believe them. "Not a murderer of any kind."

Gretchen cocks her head, eyeing him curiously. "You know, it's a little hard to take you seriously when your face is covered in lipstick."

"What?" James swipes a palm over his face, missing the biggest smear by half an inch. "Where?" He turns and frowns in the mirror by the door, then makes an exasperated noise. "Was someone going to tell me?"

Lily shrugs and turns with her tissue to mop her handiwork off his face. Gretchen regards me with a curious look. "Not a very good friend, Gabe. Letting your pal walk around with lip prints on his face?"

"I'm kind of an asshole." Might as well put it out there.

Gretchen smiles. "In that case, should I rescind my dinner offer?"

"No soup for you," I quip, doing my best imitation of the Soup Nazi from *Seinfeld*.

Gretchen blows a strand of hair off her forehead with a vaguely sheepish expression. "Okay, I'm guessing that's a movie reference."

"Television, actually." Wait, she's never heard of the Soup Nazi?

"I don't watch that, either."

"What?"

She shrugs, hands fisted in her hoodie pockets. "Movies, TV—any of it. I don't even own a television."

I've never heard of such a thing. "Are you Amish?"

She laughs and shakes her head. "I'm a research scientist. And a PhD candidate. And a professor. Not a lot of time in there to add TV junkie to the list."

Lily finishes swiping the lipstick off James's face and turns to join our conversation. "We're sort of hoping once she finishes her dissertation, she'll become one of us," she says. "Binge-watching *Grey's Anatomy* and *Stranger Things* over large quantities of wine."

"Dare to dream." Gretchen holds up the dill and takes a step back. "I'd better finish my chowder. Gabe—come on over when you're ready. It's the cabin next door. Jon and Blanka's place."

I know I should get on the road. I've got a ninety-minute

drive ahead of me. This is my chance to back out. To be alone. To get in my car and drive far, far away.

But as I look at Gretchen, I know I'd walk on my lips across crushed ice to eat a bowl of cold oatmeal with her.

"I'll be right over."

CHAPTER 2

GRETCHEN

*O*h, dear God. Did I really just invite a strange man to dinner?

Admittedly, it's been a slow stretch of months since I accepted the adjunct professor role at OSU Cascades. Between lecturing and researching and grading papers, my lone foray into dating was a disaster.

Besides, the little apartment I rented next to campus came equipped with a homebody roommate, which is why I jumped at the chance to house sit for my brother.

There's no roommate here. Just five cats—Jessica, Sinbad, Raisin, Eloise, and Zinnia—lined up in a judgmental row as I walk into the kitchen.

"Stop looking at me like that," I tell them as I pry the lid off the bubbling pot of chowder. Warm steam billows out, and I breathe in the scent of winter afternoons at my grandma's place on the Oregon Coast. Red potatoes simmer beside bright bits of carrot and corn, swirling with plump, pink salmon chunks. I give the whole thing a stir before adding a pinch of salt.

I look up to see the cats still staring at me. "What?" I tap the spoon on the side of the pot as Jessica twitches her whiskers in silent judgment. "So I invited a guy over for dinner. I was just being friendly."

The cats are unconvinced. Or maybe they're hungry. But I fed them an hour ago, so I'm pretty sure they're judging.

I focus on Jessica, mother and ringleader of the motley bunch. With her gnarled stump tail and scarred face, she holds the unofficial record as the world's homeliest cat. Her massive polydactyl paws complete the picture of an animal raised next to a nuclear power plant.

She continues to stare, her eerie green eyes indicating she's unimpressed by me. "He's a friend of James and Lily," I explain. "It's not like I'm dragging a stranger home from the bar. And he's nothing like Alastair."

Like I'd know. I spent five minutes with Gabe. I've had longer interactions with the guy who writes parking tickets on campus.

Jessica sighs and closes one eye. Beside her, Zinnia twitches her tail and rearranges her body into a donut shape. Even Sinbad looks dubious.

"Oh, come on." The words come out strangely shouty, and I tap the spoon on the pot again, spattering my hand with chowder. "It's not like I invited him over to bang me on the kitchen counter."

"Gretchen?"

I snap my head up, and there he is in the doorway. Gabe whats-his-name in all his six-two, red-scarfed, tousle-haired glory. He looks like the product of a cloning experiment between a hot professor and an underwear model, and I pray to God he didn't hear those last few words.

"I'm sorry." He's frozen on the welcome mat, brown eyes wide with uncertainty. "I thought I heard you yell 'come in.' I can go back outside and—"

"No, *no*—it's fine." Heat rushes my face, and I wonder if I can blame it on the steam from the soup. I give it another good stir, needing something to do with my hands. "I was just talking to the cats."

"Wow." He surveys the lineup, and I watch the words 'crazy cat lady' race through his mind.

"They're not mine," I assure him. "They're what happens when a soft-hearted humanitarian accidentally adopts a pregnant stray."

He smiles, and I notice a dimple in his left cheek. "The soft-hearted humanitarian would be your brother?" He unwinds the scarf from his neck, which I take as a sign he plans to stay. "I've met Jon a few times. James said you're pet sitting?"

"For a couple weeks, yes." I nod to the hook beside the door. "You can hang up your coat there. Can I get you a glass of wine? I've got a Pinot Noir open, but there's Pinot Gris in the fridge."

He drapes his coat on the hook and moves to the other side of the kitchen island. His stride is long and confident, and I try not to stare as he folds his oversized frame onto a barstool and rests his hands on the counter. My gaze snags on his hands. They're big and rugged, a contrast to his expensive shoes and a sweater that looks like it cost more than my last year of grad school.

I'm staring at his hands, wondering what he does for a living. I could ask, but it seems tasteless to interrogate the guy before the ice chips melt from his hair.

"Water would be great," he says, reminding me I've offered him a beverage. "Or juice or soda or whatever."

"Oh." Shit. Did I just offer booze to a recovering alcoholic? Leave it to me to stick a foot in it with the first hot guy I've dined with since—

"Water, yes, hang on." I look down and remember I've slopped soup over my knuckles. "Let me get the chowder off my hand."

"I've got it." He stands up, and for one absurd moment, I think he intends to lick soup off my knuckles. I'm good with that. "Which cupboard are the glasses in?"

My fingers sting from the heat of the soup, and my face burns from the shame of my own awkwardness. "Right next to the fridge," I tell him. "Icemaker's in the door."

"I'm on it." He moves around the counter and gets his own glass of water while I try to regroup. Stirring the chowder again seems like a good start.

"I'm not an alcoholic," he says as he eases himself back onto the barstool. "I'm assuming that's why you got all flustered?"

I got flustered because I don't normally invite stupid-hot men to dinner, but I nod anyway. "Right. I mean—good. That's good that you're not." Did that sound judgey? "Not that there's anything wrong with that. I work in academia, so not much shocks me."

He stares at me for a long time. An uncomfortably long time, which has me stirring the soup harder. I glance down to see I've made a spinning whirlpool of salmon and potato chunks, and I order myself to put the spoon down.

"I'm driving tonight," he says. "That's why I'm not drinking. But you go right ahead."

"Already on it." I lift my glass in a shaky toast, then feel the need to clarify. "I'm not an alcoholic, either. Just killing the bottle before I leave."

"You're going somewhere?"

I didn't mean to say that. It's not smart to tell a strange man I'm en route to a remote cabin in the woods to work on my dissertation. True, we established he's not a serial killer, but did Ted Bundy go around advertising it?

"My brother's coming back," I tell him, thinking fast. "They're visiting our parents in Europe, but they fly home tomorrow."

"And you go back to your place?"

I decide that's a rhetorical question, so I'm not technically lying when I nod. "Soup's just about ready. Oh! I forgot the bread."

Gabe glances at the clock on the wall. "I could see if they have some at the lodge. They should still be open, and it's just across the way."

"No, I made sourdough." I nod at the bread machine tucked next to the fridge. "Well, Giancarlo made bread."

"Giancarlo?"

I ladle soup into bowls, careful not to splash my hand this time. "I name all my household appliances. It makes me feel rich and exotic to say, 'Giancarlo is home baking bread,' or 'Louise made me this amazing pork roast.'"

"And Louise is?"

"My slow cooker."

He laughs and steps around the counter to inspect the bread machine. After figuring out the latch, he pries out the sourdough and sets it on Jon's battered wooden cutting board.

"All your appliances, huh?" He looks thoughtful, and I brace myself for an awkward vibrator joke. "How about your toaster?"

"Bob Marley," I say without hesitation.

He laughs. "Toaster, toasted...stoner humor?"

"Right." I wonder if I should clarify I'm not a pothead, but that seems like overkill. I settle for sprinkling dill over the bowls while Gabe slices into the bread, releasing a fragrant cloud of yeasty goodness. My stomach rumbles, and I'm not sure if I'm hungrier for food or for the man helping me prepare it.

"How about your laptop?" He frowns. "Or do you have one?"

"I'm a college professor. I definitely have a laptop."

He smiles and keeps slicing bread. "Wasn't sure if your TV aversion extended to all screens."

"No, but I'm not on social media." I clear my throat. "Steve. My laptop is Steve." I can't tell from looking if Gabe thinks I'm adorably quirky or insane.

"Steve Jobs, I presume?" He grins. "Which means you're a Mac girl."

I'm ridiculously pleased he gets it. "I am indeed."

"I like you even more than I did five minutes ago."

For some reason, that perfectly platonic compliment sends a frizzle of joy through me. I keep my eyes averted, concentrating on getting out silverware while Gabe finishes slicing bread and loads it into the wooden bowl I've set beside the cutting board. I reach over to cover the bowl with a clean dishcloth, brushing his hand by accident. Sparks shoot from my wrist to my armpit, which is more pleasant than it sounds.

"I own both an ice cream maker and a milkshake machine," I blurt to distract him from the heat in my face. "Actually, two ice cream makers. One for sorbets and one that's the old-fashioned hand crank kind."

"Now you're just bragging." There's a teasing glint in his eyes, and his hand brushes mine again as he reaches past me for the butter dish. "Okay, if you were a movie girl, I'd be guessing names like George—for the scene in *It's a Wonderful Life* where young George Bailey bonds with his future wife in an ice cream parlor."

"I actually *have* seen that film, but no."

He looks pensive as he carries the bread to the table and returns for the napkins and silverware. "Wait, no—you'd be more into 1979's *Mad Max* when Max's wife fights off a bad guy with an ice cream cone and a knee to the nuts." He snaps his fingers. "Jess—I think her name was Jess."

I'm not sure what to make of the fact that he thinks of me in the same vein as a knee to the nuts. I decide to take it as a compliment. "Never saw that one."

"Okay, I give up." He scoops up the soup bowls and carries them to the table. "What did you name your ice cream maker and milkshake machine?"

I smile as I finish tossing the arugula and pear salad. "You're actually not that far off with the pop culture stuff. The ice cream maker is Sarah."

"Sarah?"

"For that Sarah McLaughlin song from the nineties—the one about your love being better than ice cream?"

I realize before I've gotten the words out that I'm inching into flirtatious territory. I didn't mean to, but I can't help noticing my heart swaying to the beat of that sappy love song. I'm grateful his back is turned as he arranges the bowls on Jon's blue and white placemats.

"And the milkshake maker is Kelis," I add, averting my eyes as I pile the salad onto two plates.

"Ha!" He claps his hands together, striding over to grab salt and pepper and butter knives, all of which I probably would have forgotten. "For that hip-hop song by Kelis—'Milkshake,' right?"

"Right. I played it once for Jon's niece."

"Libby, right? Mark's girl?"

I'm surprised he knows this, since Mark and Chelsea have been together less than a year. Gabe must be closer to the Bracelyns than I realized.

"James keeps me up to date on family news," he says, reading my thoughts. "I haven't actually met Libby yet."

"Right. Anyway, I made a milkshake for Libby, and she went straight for the front window."

He laughs. "Was she disappointed not to see boys in the yard?"

"Not really." I pick up both salad plates and hand them to him. "Boys have cooties."

"So I've heard." His eyes crinkle at the corners, and I notice they're the most delicious blend of amber brown.

I'm a sucker for brown eyes.

I concentrate on inventorying everything on the table so I don't give in to the urge to wrap myself around him like a python. It's been more than a month since things crashed and burned with Alastair. I'm sex-starved, that's all. Nothing I can't solve with a few minutes alone with my *other* favorite appliance.

As soon as we're seated, Gabe spreads his napkin over his lap and dives into the meal. "So tell me about this cinematic aversion of yours," he says. "Is it a hard and fast rule against all television and movies, or what?"

I swallow my first bite of chowder and wash it down with the ice water that magically appeared on my place mat. Gabe sure made himself useful.

"I guess it started in grade school when I saw Bambi."

"And it scarred you for life?"

"Sort of," I admit. "When you read a sad book, you can prepare yourself mentally. But movies just hit you square in the face with dead deer. I couldn't handle it."

I'm aware that I've just confessed to a total stranger my tendency to bury my head in the sand instead of dealing with uncomfortable truths. Or maybe he didn't hear all that, what with me blathering about Bambi.

"Anyway, I never really got into visual media after that," I say. "TV and movies just took time away from studying anyway."

"And you're a researcher," he says.

How much do I love that Gabe pays attention?

"Wildlife biology is my specialty," I tell him. "I'm researching Sierra Nevada red foxes. They're a rarely seen subspecies recently found to be roaming in the Oregon Cascades."

"Not just the Sierras?"

"Nope." I blow on a spoonful of chowder. "Fewer than one hundred live in Northern California, and they're on a waiting list for protection under the Federal Endangered Species Act. But these Oregon sightings are a game changer. No one has any idea how many there could be."

I realize I'm starting to sound geeky. Gabe's probably used to women adept at discussing the latest indie films or pop culture references from TV.

But he just grins around a big bite of salad. "That's really cool. I can see why you'd pick that over being glued to a screen."

"I do have a lot more time in my day than folks with a nightly TV habit." I dab my mouth with the napkin, hoping I don't have chowder on my face. "But a lot of friends' conversations go right over my head. Someone will quote a movie or start talking about the latest season of some hit show, and I'll just be nodding along going, 'I have no idea what you're talking about.'"

He laughs and polishes off his last bite of salad. He wasn't kidding about being hungry. "You're not missing much. Trust me."

Pushing aside the salad plate, he picks up his soup spoon. I wonder if it's an etiquette thing, the ritual of polishing off one course before starting another. Maybe it's a family routine. Or maybe I should stop obsessing about the man's eating habits and focus on my own dinner.

He takes his first bite of soup and groans like I've given him a hand job under the table. "Oh my God." He slumps his shoulders, eyes glazed with pleasure. "This is amazing. Holy crap, you *made* this?"

I laugh and take another bite. It is pretty good, if I say so myself. "My grandmother used to cover it in hot sauce," I tell him. "I never realized that was weird until I got to college and tried it without. It was like a whole new world."

He laughs around another big bite of chowder, then takes a swig of water. "When I was growing up, my grandma used to eat mustard as a snack."

"Mustard?" I frown, trying to picture it. "Like on crackers or—"

"Nope, just mustard. She'd sit there with the jar of Grey Poupon and eat it by the spoonful." He shudders and eats another bite of chowder.

I file away that information, curious about his upbringing. My middle-class brain pictured a plastic squeeze bottle of French's, but Gabe grew up with Grey Poupon. That makes sense if he went to school with James. My own brother, Jon, spent his school years in fancy private academies, courtesy of his father's money.

"Do you have a big family?" I ask.

He blinks at me, visibly startled. "Why do you ask?"

I shrug and lace my fork through the leafy fronds of arugula. "Just a guess. You jumped right in and started helping in the kitchen. Kids who grow up in big families tend to do that."

There's the tiniest hint of wariness when he nods. "Yeah. Three brothers, counting me, and three sisters. How about you?"

"I'm one of six sisters," I tell him. "Plus Jonathan, who had a different dad and a zillion half-siblings on the Bracelyn side."

"And you're not related to them." He's connecting the dots, or maybe he already knew the details. "But you seem close with the family."

"The Bracelyns kinda adopted me when I visited last fall and stuck around for the teaching position. They're totally different from my family, but amazing."

"What do your parents do?"

Is it just me, or is Gabe hell-bent on peppering me with questions so he doesn't have to talk about himself? I don't mind, but I file the observation in the back of my brain.

"My mom's a retired nurse, and my dad's a retired Coast Guard Admiral," I tell him.

He takes another bite of soup and the bliss on his face leaves me tingling in spots I shouldn't think about at the dinner table. Or while talking about my parents.

"I don't think I've ever known a Coast Guard officer," Gabe says. "What's he like?"

I search my brain for another example of family quirks. Something to accompany my grandma's hot sauce and his grandma's mustard. Something to give Gabe a sense of my father's unselfconscious, easygoing nature. "When my mother would make navy bean soup, my dad would pass around the bottle of Beano like it was a condiment."

"Beano?"

Heat creeps up my throat, but I refuse to be embarrassed by introducing flatulence to our dinner conversation. "It's supposed to prevent gas," I tell him. "I never realized other families didn't do it until college when Jon invited me to this fancy dinner hosted by his brother, Sean."

"That's the Michelin starred chef brother, right?"

"Yep. And guess who has two thumbs and asked for Beano at a fancy eight-course meal?" I plant both elbows on the table and gesture to myself, earning a laugh from Gabe.

"That's awesome," he says, still laughing. "If it makes you feel better, I never knew other families watched movies in silence."

"What do you mean?"

There's that flash of wariness again. Like he's replaying his words, trying to decide if this story is okay to tell.

He seems to decide it is and keeps going. "Growing up, my whole family would sit around dissecting movies while we watched. There'd be this running commentary about the costuming or the casting choices or whether the director should have cut away a few seconds earlier." There's a light in his eyes, a warmth that tells me he's close with his family. "Anyway, I thought that's just how people watched films. I was sixteen before a friend invited me over for a *Star Wars* marathon and had to tell me to shut the fuck up halfway through the first film."

I laugh, both at the story and the fact that we've gone from farts to f-bombs already. Clearly the dinner conversation is loosening up.

Sipping my wine, I comb my brain for another family story. "My mother used to keep a beta fish in a bowl on the kitchen counter. It would die, and she'd get a new one, and she'd always name it the same thing."

Gabe looks intrigued. "Which was?"

"Master."

I wait for that to sink in. For him to nod politely or look appalled or not get it at all.

He busts out laughing. "Your mother named a fish Master Beta?"

"Multiple fish." I roll my eyes and take a sip of water. "My father was gone a lot with the Coast Guard, so she said the fish was good company. I never got it until one of my friends started snickering in high school. Suffice it to say, I was mortified."

"I think I'd like your mom."

"I think you would, too." I consider that, wondering if it's weird to be envisioning meet-the-parents scenarios when we probably won't see each other again after his chowder bowl is empty.

Speaking of which—

"Want more chowder?" I offer. "Or ice cream?"

"Ice cream?" He looks so sweetly hopeful that I'm tempted to hand him a whole gallon and a soup spoon and let him go to town.

"It's chocolate chip mint," I tell him. "My personal fave."

"Yes, please." He stands up and starts clearing the table without being asked, another point for Gabe—Gabe—crap, what's his last name?

I stand up and clear the rest of the dishes. "What did you say your last name was?"

His back is turned, and I watch him stiffen. Or maybe I'm imagining things, because he's moving toward the sink a second later. "I didn't," he says simply. "Actually, I—oh, shit."

A bowl slips from his hand and crashes onto the wood floor. The white ceramic dome splits in two, with one half shattering into a dozen sharp bits.

"Dammit, I'm so sorry." He sets the rest of the dishes on the counter and whirls around. "Is there a broom somewhere?"

"The closet behind you." My brain flashes on his expression the instant before the bowl hit the ground. It was almost like —relief?

But that can't be right.

"Let me give you cash for the bowl," he says as he drags the broom across the floor. He's not meeting my eyes, intent on scraping every last shard into the long-handled dustpan. "I know you're house sitting, and it's tough to find single bowls. They'll need a whole new set of dishes and—"

"Gabe, it's okay." I touch his arm and smile to let him know it really is. "Jon keeps a whole stash of Dollar Store dishes for when Libby comes to dinner. Or his clumsy sister, who also has a habit of breaking things." I pat his arm, conscious of the muscles under his sweater. "It's really okay; I promise."

His dubious look turns hopeful. There's something soft in his eyes, something almost...heated.

Maybe it's that I'm touching his arm. And standing close, way closer than I realized. I should step back. Or stop touching him. Or—

"Thank you," he says and covers my hand with his. "For everything."

I nod, not entirely sure what that encompasses, but knowing I like his touch. I like it way more than I should. "Don't mention it."

I look down at his hand, intrigued all over again by the size of it. "Are you a carpenter or doctor or something?" Too late, I realize those professions have little to do with one another. "Or a set builder," I add, remembering the LA reference back at James's house.

He blinks, and there's that hint of wariness again. "Why are those your guesses?"

I swallow hard, realizing how hot it is in this kitchen. Ice cream. I should definitely get the ice cream.

But I don't move. "You seem like someone who works with his hands."

He smiles, and the invisible ice cream blob in my belly becomes a puddle of melted goo. "Something like that." He squeezes my hand, which is still curled around his bicep.

Then he steps back. I drop my hand to my side, conscious of my heart skittering against the thin bones of my ribs.

"I should get that ice cream." I whirl around and contemplate sticking my head in the freezer to cool my flaming cheeks. "Three scoops or four?"

He laughs, and I hear the clatter of broken dishware hitting the trash bin. "I love that those are the options," he says. "Four, please."

"Done."

I pull the bucket out of the freezer by the handle and locate my ice cream scoop on the counter. Yes, I travel with my own. "Sadly, I don't have Dave here."

"Dave?"

"My electric ice cream scoop."

Gabe frowns, puzzling it out. "I give up. Why Dave?"

"Dave Matthews Band has a song called 'Spoon.' It's a stretch, I know."

He laughs and settles back on the barstool he occupied when he first arrived. "I can't decide if I'm more charmed by your naming conventions or that you have an actual electric ice cream scoop."

"Thank you," I tell him. "It's definitely one of my favorite appliances."

"What's your absolute favorite?"

A flood of naughty thoughts seeps into my brain. If I were Lily, I'd own it. Name the make and model of my vibrator and dare anyone to shame me for it.

If I were Jon's fiancée, Blanka, I'd launch into a scientific explanation of human arousal or pleasure aids through the centuries.

But I'm me, so I set a bowl of chocolate chip mint in front of Gabe and pick up my spoon. "It's a toss-up between my ice cream maker and my chainsaw."

"You own a chainsaw?"

"Sally." I grin a little sheepishly. "My dad came up with that one."

"From *Texas Chainsaw Massacre*?"

"Bingo." I shove a big heap of chocolate chip mint in my mouth. "I've never actually seen the movie, but I've had Sally since I was sixteen."

"You're kidding me."

I shake my head and spoon up more ice cream. "Not like I take it grocery shopping or anything, but yeah. I spent my teen years in Alaska. You learn to cut firewood young when you've only got a woodstove for heat."

I spoon another bite of ice cream into my mouth and watch Gabe for a reaction. He stares at me for a long time, then shakes his head. "You're something else," he says. "You know, earlier I was wondering what it'd be like to date you."

"Oh?" I'm trying to keep my voice casual, not to let on that this piques my interest way more than it should.

"You're not into visual media, so there'd be no dinner-and-a-movie dates," he says. "No Netflix-and-chill."

I laugh and take another bite of ice cream. "I do know what that means," I tell him. "But only because Lily explained it to Izzy last week."

"Izzy?"

"The newest Bracelyn sister. I'm guessing you haven't met her. They just found her a few months ago. She's from this tiny country in Southern Europe, and there's some serious culture shock happening."

He laughs and spoons up a generous dip of ice cream. "I take it she didn't know Netflix and chill was a euphemism for sex?"

"Nope." I laugh around my spoon. "Which made it awkward when she invited Libby the seven-year-old to do it with her. I was all for it, thinking we'd do this fun cartoon marathon or something. Lily had to take us aside and explain."

Gabe laughs and scrapes the bottom of his ice cream bowl. I'm surprised to discover how bummed I am that we're reaching the end. Of this meal, this conversation…everything.

He stands up and rinses his bowl. "Once my grandmother

caught my sister Lana flipping off my other sister Lauren."

"Your sisters are named Lana and Lauren?"

He nods, not meeting my eyes. "And Marilyn, but she goes by Mari."

I chew on that tidbit, pretty sure those are all movie star names from the forties and fifties. "Your parents must have liked old movies."

He looks at me, then nods once. "Yeah. They do." He looks down to load his bowl and spoon in the dishwasher. "Anyway, Lana flipped Lauren the bird this one time. When Grandma saw it, Lana convinced her it was sign language for 'I love you.'"

"No way."

Gabe puts a hand over his heart. "Swear to God. For almost a year, Grandma said goodbye at the door by flashing her middle finger at us."

I bust out laughing, delighted with this sliver of information about his life. "That's fabulous," I tell him. "Your family sounds like a kick."

"Yeah," he says softly. "They are."

Something's shifted between us. I'm not sure what it is, but it feels like intimacy mixed with melancholy. His brown eyes meet mine and hold for a good long time. I'm not sure what's happening, but I don't want it to stop.

When he speaks, his voice is velvet soft. "I should go."

"All right." I try not to sound disappointed. "It's been nice having you here."

"This was amazing." He pushes away from the counter, putting space between us. "One of the best nights of my life."

I study his face and wonder if he's teasing. He doesn't look like it. If I didn't know better, I'd almost think he's as sad as I am about saying goodbye.

"Drive safely." I comb my brain for something else to say. For some excuse to keep him here in this warm kitchen talking about families and work and childhood memories.

There's a look in his eyes that tells me I'm not alone. That if I asked, he might just stay.

Knock it off.

I shake my head, forcing the thought from my brain. That's insane. I've known him a few hours, and I'm just getting over an ugly breakup.

Wriggling myself out of the lust-haze, I extend a hand. "It's been great meeting you, Gabe."

He nods, his fingers warm and big around mine. "Likewise."

I don't volunteer my phone number. He doesn't ask for it. I know this is how it has to be. He's only passing through, and I'm still a mess from how badly things ended with Alastair.

That doesn't mean it feels great to let go of his hand.

Gabe steps back. "Better hit the road."

He stares at me for another long moment. Then he turns and heads for the door. I watch as he drapes the red scarf around his neck and sets to work buttoning and zipping. I stand there twisting a dish towel in my hands, not sure if I should go hug him or wave goodbye from here.

"Drive carefully." I already said that, didn't I?

"I will." He holds my gaze from across the room. It feels like five inches separating us, maybe less. "Thanks again for dinner. And for the great company."

"Don't mention it."

Again, he hesitates. I consider channeling my inner Lily. Offering my number or maybe flashing my boobs.

"Take care," Gabe says.

Then he twists the knob and slips out.

I stare at the door as it closes, surprised to feel a sinking in my gut. It was just dinner. It was fun, it was friendly, and that's all. The last thing I need right now is another romantic entanglement with a guy I know nothing about. Been there, done that, burned the T-shirt.

Pushing off the counter, I stride toward the door to lock the deadbolt. As my fingertips touch cold metal, the door flies open.

"I'm sorry." Gabe steps through with icy air swirling in behind him. His brown eyes are bright and clear.

"You forgot something?" I glance around for a missing glove, but Gabe grabs my hand.

"This was the nicest evening I've had in years, and I'll probably regret kissing you, but I'd regret it more if I didn't." He pauses, still gripping my hand. "And now I regret saying that out loud."

My heart thuds in my ears as the cold makes my nipples tighten. Or maybe it's not the cold. I grip Gabe's hand in mine. "You seem to have a lot of regrets."

"You have no idea." He lets go of my hand and slides his arms around my waist. "Can I kiss you?"

I nod and lick my lips. "Wouldn't want you leaving with regrets."

And then his lips are on mine. He's slow at first, soft and gentle. A gust of cold air blasts us from the side, and I lift my slipper to kick the door closed. Gabe deepens the kiss, fingers sliding into my hair. He unfurls my messy bun, his mouth tasting like mint and snowfall and no trace of regret.

When he draws back, my heart's drumming so hard I'm sure he hears it. The smile he gives me could melt the frost off a windshield.

"Take care, Gretchen."

This time when he leaves, I know it's for good. I watch his shadow move down the pathway, across the lawn toward James's cabin. It's too dark to see his car, but I watch the headlights flick on, watch the shadowy shape back out in a perfect three-point turn. Tiny ice flecks dance through yellow beams as his taillights drift down the driveway.

I watch until the lights vanish, waiting for my heart to stop pounding.

It's another hour before that happens.

CHAPTER 3

GABLE

I think about Gretchen for the whole ninety-minute drive to the cabin. The roads aren't bad, so it's safe to let my mind wander.

God, that felt amazing.

Not just the kiss, though yeah…that was incredible.

But more amazing was the conversation with someone who didn't know me. Not from television or movies or from fiery, furious headlines.

Hollywood icon embroiled in scandal.

I wonder if Gretchen knows about it. Even if she didn't connect the dots to me, she must have seen a newspaper headline or something. Some tidbit of gossip passed like dirty candy on the internet.

Grieving families file suit against Gable Judson.

I look down to see my knuckles have gone white on the steering wheel. I order myself to relax as the GPS guides me off the paved road and onto the rugged gravel leading the final four miles to the cabin. The forest is thick here with shaggy pines hunched so close together their ice-coated needles touch.

As my headlights cut a swath of yellow through the trees,

something skitters across the road. A bobcat, maybe? Or one of Gretchen's foxes.

Everything leads my thoughts back to her. I know I wasn't imagining the energy between us. She felt it, too, that "hello, there" sense of knowing someone on a bone-deep level even if you've just met.

Corny, I know. What can I say? My favorite films have always had threads of romance. Maybe the chemistry with Gretchen was all in my head. Or maybe she was being kind, helping out a friend of the family.

Even if that's true, it was nice talking to her. To feel like a regular guy having dinner with a regular girl.

She's no regular girl.

It's true she's something special. I loved her cleverness. Her quickness to laugh. All those things made me want to stay in that warm, cedar-scented kitchen forever. I loved her comfy gray sweatpants and the fact that she didn't rush to put on makeup like my sisters do when someone comes to dinner. I get it, I do—Hollywood's a bastard to women, and my sisters have to play the game just like the rest of us.

Which I guess is what I love so much about Gretchen. She's so far removed from my Hollywood life that she may as well exist on another planet. A planet I'd desperately love to visit.

My headlights flash across the small cabin, and I hit the brakes. It's just like James described it, with a red metal roof and a deck that wraps all the way around the side. In the shadows of the front porch, I spot the pile of neatly stacked firewood.

I step out of the car and stretch the kinks out of my back, breathing in crisp night air that tastes like pine. It's colder up here than at the resort, with patchy spots of snow covering the ground in places the sun can't reach. An owl hoots somewhere in the distance, but other than that, it's silent. Silent and completely, totally isolated.

I feel my shoulders start to relax for the second time in weeks.

The first was back in Gretchen's kitchen, but here I'm practically melting with relief. The cool air draws the darkness out of me, muffling the shouts of headlines and phone calls and cacophony of noises filling my head in recent weeks.

So this is what peace feels like. I could get used to it.

I spend an hour hauling in my clothes and coolers and boxes of food. The cabin's tiny and every bit as rustic as James warned last week when I called.

"Are you certain you don't want one of our luxury cabins at the resort?" he asked. "Radiant floor heat, jacuzzi tubs, gas fireplaces that turn on with the flip of a switch."

"I've had enough luxury," I told him. "I'm looking for rustic."

Rustic and isolated, which this place is. I run a hand over the knotty wood paneling, then check out the wood stove that serves as the sole source of heat. It's been cleaned recently, even though I told James I was fine with a little dust.

Shoving my jacket into the coat closet, I wander to the only other interior door in the place. It's a bathroom the size of a postage stamp with a small shower and vanity and toilet.

Back in the small kitchen, I run a hand over the gnarled juniper countertop and survey the rest of the one-room cabin. There's a queen-sized bed piled high with crisp patchwork quilts. Probably from the craft market in town, just like the red and white checkered throw pillows plumped at the edges of a worn leather couch. In the breakfast nook off the kitchen, two chairs and a small table wait expectantly by a big window.

It's perfect.

Yawning, I let my gaze stray to the bed. How long has it been since I slept through the night? Days. Weeks. Maybe longer.

But I can't sleep yet. Fire first, since the cabin is freezing. Trudging back out onto the porch, I haul in enough wood to get things going. My chest burns with appreciation for the well-stocked woodpile. I know I've been an asshole these past weeks.

Maybe longer, and I'm grateful for friends and family who have my back.

Back inside, I blow on the tiny embers until flames roar to life. I add a couple big logs, hoping that lasts through the night. Closing the door, I sit back on my heels and take a breath.

Now I can rest.

But I can't. Like an idiot, I plunk down on the sofa and pull out my phone. There's no service out here, so it's just a dumb habit. Besides, the last thing I want is to be buried in a barrage of messages.

Are you okay?

Gable, we need to talk.

It wasn't your fault.

But now my phone screen is blank. Just the spot in the top left corner indicating zero bars for service.

Perfect.

I power off and make a mental note to drive to town tomorrow to let James and Lily know I'm here. I texted them when I passed through, so they know I made it that far. When this is over, I'll have to remember to do something nice for them. A case of wine or maybe industrial-strength lipstick remover.

I don't realize I'm smiling until Gretchen's face flashes in my mind.

That kiss. My God. Soft and sweet and hungry and passionate and everything a first kiss should be but almost never is.

Part of me wishes I'd gotten her number. Most of me knows it's for the best that I didn't.

If she had any idea who I am—what I've done—she'd never talk to me again. Better to leave with her thinking I'm a regular guy with good table manners and a normal family. It's easier that way.

I glance at my watch, surprised to realize it's nearly midnight. The room is toasty and smells like woodsmoke, so I force myself to leave the couch and pry off my boots and flannel shirt.

Recalling something I read about body heat circulating better without clothes, I strip off my jeans and sweater and T-shirt, leaving me in boxers and socks.

Then I burrow into the deep puddle of quilts and pull the covers over my head. I know I should brush my teeth. I know I should stoke the fire. I know I should do a lot of things I've failed to do in my life.

But right now, nothing in the world sounds as wonderful as sleep.

Sleep and the woman whose face hovers behind my eyelids as I drift into a peaceful oblivion.

* * *

"GET UP."

I force my eyes open, fighting through the soupy fog of sleep to figure out where the hell I am. There's a mountain of blankets piled over my head, with a thin thread of daylight shimmering between two of the quilts.

How long have I been out?

Wait, no. That's not the question.

Who found me?

"I'm going to count to ten." A trickle of fear slides down my spine as the intruder speaks again. Female, I realize as my brain wakes up. "And I want you to come out nice and slow with your hands up."

That voice. I blink again, pretty sure I'm imagining it. Or projecting maybe, since I spent the night dreaming of Gretchen in her warm, cozy kitchen.

She's not really here. She can't be.

"Ten." Her voice is clear and calm, with no trace of humor. "Nine." Another long pause. "Eight."

"Wait." I stick my hands out of the covers, heart drumming in my ears. I have no idea what's happening, but I'm not eager to face it in my boxer shorts. "I'm unarmed. And un-pantsed. Any chance you'd let me get dressed?"

"No." There's a distinct click, a sound I recognize from every action hero standoff scene I've watched. All the blood drains from my head.

A gun. Holy shit, she has a gun.

My agent warned me. Something about violent messages in an online forum, but he swore it was nothing. Just talk, not a real threat.

"Seven." Another pause. "Six."

Struggling to keep my voice as calm as hers, I wiggle my fingers in a ridiculous gesture that's half surrender, half cheerful wave. "Look, whoever you are, I haven't seen your face yet." It's hard to breathe under here, or maybe I'm starting to hyperventilate. "My wallet's on the counter. Just take what you want and go."

There's a long silence. She's stopped counting, which is a good sign. "Are you serious?"

A burst of laughter cracks the silence, and I know. I *know* it's her.

Gretchen.

I throw back the covers and stare at the woman who dominated my dreams all night. She wears jeans and a red and pink flannel over a white tee. Her caramel hair is loose around her shoulders and topped with a tasseled pink hat.

It's such a contrast to the pistol in her hand that I almost laugh out loud.

"What the—" Gretchen gasps as the quilts slip down around my waist. Her eyes drop to my bare chest and linger a few beats before she lowers the gun. "Holy shit."

"That's my line." I squint against the glare of sunlight streaming through the windows, struggling to focus on her face. "What are you doing here?" A ripple of panic moves through me. "Wait, did something happen to James and Lily?"

"James and Lily?" All at once, Gretchen's eyes go wide. "Oh my God. They loaned you the cabin?"

I'm grateful she figured it out, since my sleep-sluggish brain is still dog paddling through molasses to get to shore. Slowly, the pieces fall into place. "I'm going to go out on a limb and say James guessed wrong when he said none of the other siblings remembered this place." I study her face, and my heart wobbles as those sea glass eyes sweep my chest again. "I'm thinking at least one sibling does."

Gretchen shakes her head, as dumbfounded as I feel. "Jonathan said their dad won it in a poker game. That no one ever used it, so it'd be the perfect place for me to hole up and work on my dissertation." She fishes a key out of her pocket and holds it up. "He gave it to me before they left for Europe."

"Christ." I glance at the gun in her hand, not sure whether to laugh or be freaked out. At least she's not pointing it at me anymore. I lift my eyes to her face, and there's that heart wobble again. "Can I please put on my pants now?"

"Oh. Yes, sorry." She flips the safety, then sets the gun on the counter behind her. "You scared me."

"I know the feeling." Snaking my hand out of the covers, I manage to snag both my pants and T-shirt.

Gretchen blushes and turns around while I tug my clothes on and stand up. I know I shouldn't check out her ass, but the jeans she's wearing fit like someone molded them to her curves. Last night's sweatpants gave me few clues about her figure, but it's clear from these jeans that Gretchen has a rockin' body.

"All right, I'm decent." I'm still buckling my belt as she turns, and her blush goes a shade deeper. "How about I make us some coffee so we can figure out how to handle this. I guess one of us will need to hit the road."

Her brows furrow. "Have you looked outside lately?"

"I've been a little preoccupied with being held at gunpoint." I shift my gaze to the window and gape at the ocean of white.

"Holy crap. When did that happen?" Stepping up to the window, I press my fingers against the glass like a kid on a snow day.

Not that we had any where I grew up.

"It started less than an hour ago," she says. "It's about five inches now but piling up fast."

I stare at my car, which looks like a fuzzy frost turtle. There's no metal visible at all. I turn back to Gretchen, who's got her hands in the back pockets of her jeans.

"I thought this wasn't supposed to hit until tonight," I say.

"Same." She shrugs. "I guess the weather guy was wrong. I figured I had plenty of time to get here and get settled."

I drag my hands through my hair and glance at the wood stove. The log inside is barely smoldering, so I should deal with getting us a heat source.

"I'll work on the fire," Gretchen says, reading my mind. "You figure out the coffee situation."

"Bathroom first." My mouth feels like something crawled inside and died. I could use a shower, but I'll settle for washing my face. "Give me two minutes."

Or longer, since the morning wood I woke up with is refusing to go down. Must be the adrenaline. I turn toward the bathroom, mustering as much dignity as possible as I close the door behind me and lock it.

Now what?

I start by splashing cold water on my face, since I'm still fighting brain fog. One glance in the mirror reminds me I look like hell, and also that the beard I grew as a disguise is threaded with salt and pepper. When did that happen?

Raking my hands through my hair again, I end up looking like I spent the night rubbing my head on the carpet. How can Gretchen look so fresh and bright and beautiful this early in the morning while I look like Wolfman's feral cousin?

Meeting my eyes in the mirror, I mouth the words that have been a constant buzz in my brain for weeks.

You are such a fuckup.

I brush my teeth, aware that I'm well over my two-minute limit. I need more time to collect myself. To figure out what we do next.

Maybe James can help me find her a cabin at the resort. Someplace pretty and private to work on her dissertation. There's obviously not room for both of us here, and the longer she sticks around, the likelier she is to figure out who I am.

My subconscious tells me I'm being a selfish prick. It's a blizzard out there, and she did get the keys before I did. I should be the one to leave.

But there are only so many places I can go and not be recognized, and besides—

"You okay in there?"

She sounds cheerful enough, but there's an edge of concern to her voice.

"I'm fine." With a sigh, I dry my face, hang up the towel, and head out to face the woman I haven't stopped thinking about since last night.

The instant I step through the door, she hands me a mug of coffee. "Here," she says. "There were enough embers to get the fire going fast, so I made the coffee, too."

I take a sip, fortified by the bitter heat of it. "This is good. Way better than the stuff I brought." I take another sip. "Did you bring your own bean grinder and fancy coffeemaker?"

She laughs and sips from her own steaming mug. "It's a French press, so not technically an appliance. But yes on grinding my own beans." Lifting the mug again, her eyes drift to the front window. "Man, it's really coming down out there."

"Right." I sigh and glance outside. Might as well take the bull by the horns. "Look, there's obviously not room for two people here. I'm not sure about the fairest way to decide who's staying, but we'd probably better do it before the roads get worse."

She gives me a curious look. "It's only four miles back to the main road," she says. "I've got chains and four-wheel drive."

"You're volunteering to leave?"

Lifting her mug, she gives me another look. "Can I finish my coffee first?"

Right. "Sorry. I'm an asshole."

"You mentioned that." She sits down on the arm of the sofa and surveys the cabin. "It really is a nice place. Those beams are beautiful."

I look up, noticing them for the first time. "Reminds me of my grandmother's place."

Gretchen smiles. "The grandma who ate mustard, or the one who flipped you off?"

I laugh and ease onto one of the barstools, glancing out the window again. The snow really is breathtaking, white and fluffy and drifting like bits of white fur.

"The mustard grandma is the one with the cabin." I can't believe I told her that story. It's not like me to open up so easily.

She doesn't even know your name. Don't go patting yourself on the back.

I clear my throat. "Look, it doesn't feel right having you just leave. Maybe there's a fairer way to decide."

Gretchen blows on her coffee. "What do you suggest?"

"Flipping a coin? Rock paper scissors?"

She just laughs. "It's not a big deal. I was actually planning to spend part of my time at the old BONK compound anyway."

"BONK?" I frown, trying to recall why that sounds familiar. "Wait—you mean the BONKers live nearby?"

"*Lived*," she says. "The Feds shut down the Benevolent Order of the New Kingdom more than a year ago. Now it's just acres of vacant buildings and one sneaky fox. Or more, we're not really sure."

Ah. I get it now. "Your fox is living at a former cult compound?"

"That's one of the areas they've had sightings." She shrugs. "The whole property has been tied up in the courts, but the Feds are letting biologists in for research. I'm supposed to head out later this week."

"It's close by?"

"About five miles north of here."

The snowstorm hurls a handful of gravelly flakes at the window, reminding me we've got bigger issues to deal with than a nearly extinct fox. "Maybe I should go."

"Go where?" She glances out the window. "I saw your car outside. Classic Mustang with rear-wheel drive?" She makes a tsk-tsk sound. "Even with chains, you're going to have a tough time getting out of here."

"I'll manage." My ego gives a tiny pinch of discomfort. I know I'm not a mountain man, but I did manage to chop kindling and get the woodstove going last night.

Gretchen polishes off her coffee and sets her mug on the counter. Then she stares at me. Just stares for an uncomfortably long time. "Is this about the kiss?"

I blink. "What?"

"You're being kind of awkward and weird." She smiles when she says it, and she's not breaking eye contact. "I'm just wondering if it's because you kissed me, and you're regretting it because you never expected to see me again."

That is literally the last thing I'd be thinking. "No," I tell her. "I definitely don't regret kissing you."

I hesitate, not sure I should put this out there.

But hell, we've already established one of us is leaving. "Frankly, I haven't stopped thinking about that kiss. That's kinda why one of us needs to leave."

"Oh." She gives a funny little smile. "Thanks for the honesty."

"Don't mention it."

I'm such a dick.

But Gretchen's smile makes me hate myself a little less. "Seriously, I'm fine being the one to leave," she says. "They have tons of cabins out at the BONK compound. I'll just stay there."

I cast another glance at the snowstorm. "How?"

She laughs. "This storm's barely getting started. I grew up in Alaska, remember?"

"Sally the Chainsaw. Right."

There's a flicker of surprise in her eyes. "I left the chainsaw at home, but I do have tire chains. And four-wheel drive. As long as I get back on the highway before this blizzard gets going, I'll be fine."

She steps toward the entrance as I set my mug on the counter and follow. I don't love the idea of her leaving so soon after she got here, but she makes a strong case. I step past her, headed for the big box of snack food I left by the front door. "Can I grab you—"

"Yes."

I freeze in my tracks. "What?"

She looks up at me and smiles. "You asked if you could grab me and I said yes." Her smile widens. "Was that not a complete question?"

I can't tell if she's yanking my chain. "I was offering to grab you a snack for the road."

So why am I stepping closer, moving into her orbit? And why is she looking at me with those blue eyes round and soft and full of heat?

"I'll take the snack," she says. "And also another kiss. It's only fair, since you kissed me goodbye last time."

I know this is a bad idea. A terrible idea. So why are my arms sliding around her waist, fingers slipping into her hair as I lean her back against the window by the door? "Okay."

The kiss is soft and slow and achingly deep. All the tentativeness from our first kiss is gone, replaced by something more urgent. There's a heat that wasn't there the first time, a familiarity I recognize like my own heartbeat. We've already said goodbye once, so maybe we're getting good at it.

Or maybe it's that I don't want this to be goodbye.

Gretchen sighs and moves against me, pressing closer. God, she's soft. Soft and so damn sweet. If I'm not careful, I could lose myself in—

Crack!

We spring apart, both blinking like we've been whacked with a club.

"What was that?" Gretchen breathes.

For a second, I think she's as dazed as I am by the kiss. Another loud *crack!* shakes me out of it.

I glance out the window and feel my blood go cold. "Oh, shit."

It's like watching a scene in slow motion. A towering pine sways, teetering in the wind. Snow bursts from the branches as the tree plummets toward the ground. Toward the cabin.

Toward *us*.

I hurl my body at Gretchen, knocking us away from the window and through the door of the open coat closet. We hit the ground hard, a pile of jackets landing on top of us as I shield her with my body and pray the tree doesn't crash through the roof.

Ka-thud!

I sit up, blinking, as Gretchen sputters beneath me. "What on earth?"

We scramble to our feet and press our faces against the window. Outside, the tree lies sprawled behind her car. Branches sway in a mist of glittery snowflakes.

"We're all right." I swallow hard, not positive it's true. "We're okay."

Gretchen nods, eyes wide as she drags her gaze off the tree and looks at me. "We're also trapped."

Right. There's that.

CHAPTER 4

GRETCHEN

I stare at Gabe, heart thudding in my ears. "You just saved my life."

He glances out the window at the tree. "Technically, the wind did that. And we don't know if it would have come through the roof or window or—"

"It would have." I swallow hard, aware of my hands shaking. "Big tree, small cabin—it's basic physics."

Even if a sharp breeze gets credit for changing the course of the tree's descent, Gabe gets credit for quick thinking. I would have just stood there like a damn lump, too mind-whacked from the kiss to think about getting out of the damn way.

"You didn't hit your head, did you?" He looks in my eyes like he's assessing me for a concussion, and my insides go melty at the gold flecks swimming in pools of mahogany. "I tried to cushion you with my arm, but the floor's pretty hard."

"No, I'm good." I rub the back of my head, though I'm positive my dizziness has nothing to do with our landing. "Thank you."

He nods and glances out the window at the toppled pine, staring it down as though the strength of his gaze might force it upright again.

41

But it lies there like a defeated giant, branches stretched as though reaching to touch the trunk of my car. My heart's pounding so hard I'm afraid it might crack my ribs. I'm starting to shake, which must mean the shock's wearing off.

"Hey." Gabe slides a hand around my hip and pulls me to him. "It's okay. We're safe."

Somehow that makes me shake harder. I'm afraid I might start crying, but the next sound that slips out is even worse.

"Are you laughing?" Gabe draws back and looks down at me. "I know shock does weird things to people, but—"

"Sorry, I'm okay." I step away from him, accepting the fact that I'm never going to get my heart rate under control with him touching me. "I can't believe it missed the cabin."

"That was crazy. It was headed right for us." He reaches for the doorknob, and I follow, crossing my fingers no more trees topple.

The snow is already past our ankles as we reach the back of my Subaru. "Damn." I rub the needles with bare fingers, still shaking. "How did that not crush my car?"

Not that it matters. It's right behind me, which still means we're stuck.

Gabe looks at me. "You said you didn't bring Sally the Chainsaw?"

I shake my head. "Just an axe."

"And a gun." It's his turn for the head shake. "Not that we're going to blast our way out of here, but I'm impressed you're so well-prepared."

I grimace. "Sort of. I was prepared for firewood and intruders. Not a stint as a lumberjack."

"That's a pretty big tree."

I shiver, conscious of how close we came to dying. And also, how close I'm standing to Gabe. He's like a human furnace, hot and solid and deliciously male.

"We should get back inside," he says. "In case more trees come down."

"Right." I follow him into the cabin, struggling to formulate a plan. "I have snowshoes. I could get back out to the highway and—"

"With trees flopping around out there?"

"Fair point." I glance out the window. "And this snow's not letting up. Not ideal conditions for snowshoeing."

Gabe's watching me, brown eyes calm and even. My heart ticks up again, but it's nothing to do with our near-death experience. It's Gabe, strong and solid and molten eyed beside me.

"You sure you're okay?" he asks softly. "You got kind of a frantic look just then."

"I'm good." I swallow hard, willing myself not to get lost in those eyes. Not to pull a repeat performance of what happened with Alastair.

Focus on survival. Not on getting laid.

"How much food do you have?" I ask.

"Enough that we won't need to go all Donner Party just yet." He shrugs. "I brought plenty. I was planning on being out here a week."

"Same."

Which also means it could be a while until anyone comes looking for us. I stare at the fallen tree and shiver. "So we really are stuck."

"Looks that way." Gabe shoves his hands in his pockets. "I guess it could be worse. We've got food and shelter and running water. Firewood for heat."

As I look into Gabe's brown eyes, my brain skitters toward thoughts of other kinds of heat. "No."

Gabe blinks. "No what?"

I didn't mean to say that out loud. "Nothing. It's just—I've made some less-than-awesome decisions."

"Oookay." He looks at me a long moment. "Did I speak too soon on the Donner Party thing?"

I laugh and force myself to push all thoughts of Alastair out of my head. "It's not that. Never mind." My stomach growls, and I'm grateful for the distraction. "Are you hungry?"

Not waiting for an answer, I move toward the kitchen. Gabe follows. "You don't have to cook for me again."

"I know I don't. But all I had was a granola bar on the drive out. I'm ready for some real breakfast."

And for some space between Gabe and me. I focus on pawing through the food box I plunked on the counter. That was before the sight of a strange man in bed transformed me from happy homesteader to ninja warrior.

I dig out a can of corned beef hash and the jumbo pack of farm fresh eggs I picked up when I stopped in town to text my brother. How soon until he and James discover the mix-up?

It could be a while. I asked Jon to keep it quiet, not wanting word to get out about the research. Nothing like a sighting of a nearly endangered animal to bring crowds of lookie-loos. Besides, I didn't want anyone at the university to hear about my solo trip. Not that I expected Alastair to show up, but—

"You really did bring a lot of food." I plop a cast iron pan on the gas stove and flip through a cupboard, determined to get my mind off my ex. "You're a fan of Dinty Moore Beef Stew, I see."

Gabe smiles and moves into the too-small kitchen. "Seemed like the sort of thing a guy should eat while staying in a rustic mountain cabin."

His expression is almost boyish, and I can't help smiling back. "My dad used to bring this anytime we'd go camping."

"I've never been camping."

"Seriously?"

"Nope. Never." His gaze sweeps the cabin, his expression almost wistful. "This is the closest I've come."

I dump the can of corned beef hash into the pan and give it a stir. "This stuff was my mom's go-to dish on snow days." The hash is sizzling now, and I add a generous dose of pepper. "As soon as we'd get the message that school was canceled, she'd make us corned beef hash and eggs before sending us out to play in the snow."

Gabe's so quiet behind me that I turn to look. He's staring at my ass, and when he lifts his gaze, he's caught somewhere between sheepishness and longing. "I never had snow days," he says. "Growing up in Southern California—" He trails off there, then shrugs. "Anyway, I missed out on a few things."

I glance down at his right hand, surprised to see he's gripping an ax. "Is this revenge for holding you at gunpoint?"

He laughs and hoists it to his shoulder. "I was going to split a little more kindling. I kept it inside last night in case an axe murderer showed up."

"And forgot his weapon, so he needed to borrow yours?"

He grins, and my insides puddle again. "Nothing more desperate than a weaponless axe murderer."

He pivots and walks out of the kitchen. A rush of cold skims the back of my neck, and I'm not sure if it's from the front door opening or from Gabe not being near me anymore. Either way, I keep my eyes on the pan, stirring the hash as it starts to crisp.

But no matter how focused I am on breakfast, I can't stop thinking about last night's kiss. And the kiss this morning, the one *I* initiated.

That was dumb. Really dumb.

In my defense, I thought we were saying goodbye for good. I had every intention of jumping in my car and driving away, never to see Gabe again. In that scenario, it seemed reasonable to claim one more kiss to cement the other in my brain. The first one happened so fast, and I spent the whole night tossing in bed, wondering if I imagined it. Trying to convince myself it couldn't possibly have been as mind-bending as I remembered.

I was wrong. If anything, the second time was better. More

familiar, more like we recognized each other on some raw, primal level.

This is how you got into trouble before.

I hate that my subconscious has a point. Following my libido instead of my ability to think things through analytically; that's where I went wrong with Alastair. If I'd taken just a few minutes to research and find out—

"Hey, Gretchen?"

Gabe's voice jolts me from the memory, and I look down to see the hash smoking on one edge of the pan.

"Yeah?" I call, scraping at the pan.

"Did you leave Sarah sitting on the ground out here?"

My flutter of joy that he remembers the name of my ice cream maker is zapped dead by another emotion. "Oh, crap. I tried to grab it on my first trip in, but my arms were full."

"I see." He's kind enough not to mention the fact that holding him at gunpoint prevented my speedy return for the appliance. "I'm sorry to deliver the news, but I think Sarah was a casualty of the Great Tree Crash of 2020."

I gasp and drop the spatula. "What?"

Gabe moves solemnly like an officer delivering news of a fallen soldier. He holds out the wreckage of metal and wood and lays it gently on the counter. "Sorry. Maybe we can fix it?"

I stare at what's left of my ice cream maker. The wooden bucket is reduced to kindling, and the metal canister inside is crushed beyond recognition. It's amazing Gabe even recognized it as an ice cream maker.

"I'm sorry for your loss." His voice is soft and low, and I look up to see he's not smiling at all. He really does mean it.

"Thank you." I bite my lip. "It's not a family heirloom or anything. I've only had this Sarah a couple years."

"I see. So Sarahs are replaceable?"

"Sort of." I glance at the wreckage of this one. "At least it wasn't Genevieve."

"Genevieve?"

"My sorbet maker. That was a gift from my late grandmother." I touch the crushed edge of Sarah's crank. "Damn."

"And now you don't have ice cream."

The solemnity of Gabe's voice is a good indication he knows this is the biggest tragedy of all. I turn back to the stove, annoyed to discover the hash smoking again. "Argh." I snatch the spatula and scrape the edges of the pan. It's only burned in a few spots, so I stir it around and hope it mixes okay with the unburned stuff. "It'll just be a little smokier than normal."

"Perfect," Gabe says. "It'll be my introduction to campfire cuisine."

"Way to look on the bright side." That, along with the tenderness he showed Sarah, is making my heart melt.

Don't get all mushy. You hardly know the guy.

But I can't help stealing looks at him as I finish off the breakfast with a couple over easy eggs while Gabe stacks wood in the living room. I try to recall what he said he does for a living. Set designer or something? It makes sense he'd be good with his hands.

As I carry the plates to the table, Gabe washes up at the kitchen sink.

"Where'd you learn to make fires like that?" I ask. "If you didn't grow up camping, I mean. Did you have a woodstove at home?"

He smiles and drops into the chair beside me, eyeing the breakfast like a starving man. "Nah, I watched a lot of *Survivor* and *Naked and Afraid*." Picking up his fork, he regards me with an odd look. "Those are reality TV shows."

"About making fire?" I have actually heard of *Survivor*, but the other one sounds suspiciously like porn.

He laughs and digs into the food. "About surviving outdoors for prolonged periods. Making fire is one of the most important skills, so I studied up."

For some reason I find this intensely charming. "How do you study making fire?"

"YouTube videos, mostly." His grin is completely unselfconscious as he stabs his fork into the center of his egg, making yellow goo ooze out. "My sister has one of those chimenea things —sort of an outdoor fire pit? So I've practiced with hers."

"You're close with your siblings?"

"Yeah. Very." He stares down at his plate like he's deciding something. When he looks up again, there's an openness in his eyes I've never seen before. "We had sort of an unusual upbringing," he says. "We're all pretty different, but we've always had each other's backs."

I wait for him to elaborate. How did they have each other's backs? And what's an unusual upbringing? Raised in a commune? Cat-hoarding parents in tinfoil hats?

But Gabe doesn't offer more. Just stands up to refill both coffee cups before setting one beside me. "How about you?" he asks. "I know you have a big family, but are you close?"

I nod around a mouthful of egg, taking a sip of coffee to wash it down. "Very. Not just with my sisters, but with Jon's family from Mom's first marriage."

"Was that weird?" he asks. "Having one brother be part of such a—" he pauses there, probably trying to come up with a nice word to describe Jon's father.

"Rich, arrogant billionaire's collection of spawn?" I supply, grinning so he knows there's no bitterness behind the words. "Not really. Jon was always more a part of our family than that one. Mostly, I felt sorry for him."

"How so?"

I shrug and mop a forkful of hash through my eggs. "His dad was such a player. All those wives and a zillion kids with so many different women. It must have been confusing, plus I think the money ended up being more of a burden than a blessing."

Gabe studies me in silence. It occurs to me that I may have

just stepped in it. If he went to fancy prep school with James, he probably grew up with money, too.

"You're right," he says before I can apologize for the gaffe. "Sometimes money and fame are more trouble than they're worth."

Fame? I don't recall mentioning that, but Gabe's still talking. "Anyway, I guess I had a weird childhood. Tell me about snow days. I feel like I missed out."

I pop the fork in my mouth and chew, considering. "They rarely called off school in Alaska, but we'd get them more often in Washington and Oregon." I spear another hunk of hash, recalling the breathless winter mornings of my childhood. "We'd get an automated call in the morning, or sometimes the night before if the superintendent made the call early."

"And it said what—that school was just canceled?"

"Or delayed." I take a sip of coffee, remembering how my sisters and I would sit in a circle by the fireplace, crossing our fingers for a full day off. "If it got called off, my mom would come up with all kinds of fun things for us to do."

"Like what?" His eyes are bright, and his voice is like a kid at story time.

A kid with broad shoulders and toned forearms and scruff that's deliciously scratchy against my cheek.

"Outdoor stuff like making snowmen or having a snowball fight," I tell him. "Or indoor stuff like obstacle courses and craft projects where we'd make marshmallow catapults. Oh! And blanket forts." I grin, warm from the memory. "Those were my favorite."

His eyes are warm and clear, like he's wallowing in my childhood "That sounds amazing."

"It was." I make a mental note to thank my mom the next time we talk. "What about you? I know you didn't have snow days, but how did you spend sick days or weekend mornings?"

"Cartoons, mostly." He smiles. "Or movie marathons."

"Tell me you at least had the blanket forts."

He laughs and folds his arms over his chest. "I don't want to brag, but I make a pretty badass blanket fort. My brothers and sisters ceded the duty to me every time."

For some reason, I find this ridiculously sexy. Then again, he could roll naked in a pile of sawdust and grape jelly and I'd find that sexy.

I hold his gaze, trying not to melt into those brown eyes. "You'll have to show me your skills sometime."

Gabe grins. "Maybe so." Unfolding his arms, he takes a sip of coffee. "So did you not watch TV at all? After the great Bambi tragedy, I mean?"

I shrug, trying to remember. "Sometimes my sisters would watch cartoons. Not much, though. My mom kept us busy with creative projects or playing outside—things like that."

"Sounds so healthy."

"She's a nurse." I smile and sip my coffee. "She read a lot of articles about the dangers of too much screen time."

"Your mom sounds great."

"She is." I laugh and swirl a forkful of hash through a puddle of egg goo. "I guess this all sounds a little hippy-dippy when I say it out loud, but I think I turned out okay."

"You turned out more than okay."

Oh, God. The low rasp of his voice, the heat in his eyes…I feel myself getting pulled in. The butterflies lying peacefully on the runway in my belly launch into a whirlwind of wings and bright color. I need to get this conversation back on safe ground before I throw myself in his lap.

"What about you?" I'm not totally sure what I'm asking, so I try again. "You said you went to school with James?"

"The last couple years of prep school," he says. "Also, the first couple years of college."

"Did you transfer or something?"

He takes another sip from his mug. "Dropped out."

There's a shuttering in his expression that tells me I've stumbled into another subject he'd rather not discuss. There seem to be a lot of those with Gabe.

But then he surprises me. "I wasn't cut out for college," he says. "And there were so many work opportunities that it seemed dumb to stick it out."

"College isn't for everyone," I say. "There's a pretty cool resurgence of graduates getting into the trades. Plumbing and electrical and construction—things like that with built-in job security."

I hold my breath, hoping that didn't sound patronizing. I don't have a clue how well set design pays, or even if he likes it.

"It was the right move for me at the time," he says. "I don't know. I guess I've been considering a change."

"Career change?" I bite my lip. "Do you know what you'd want to do?"

He shakes his head. "Not a clue. That's scary as hell, to be honest."

There's a vulnerability in his eyes that takes my breath away. If I'm not careful, I'll lose myself in this man's eyes. "I've been volunteering in the career center at the college," I tell him. "If you want, I could pull up some of the career quizzes we give to students."

He quirks an eyebrow. "This isn't an online thing, is it?"

Right. No internet. "I think I might have a printed copy. Or something I've downloaded onto my laptop."

"Steve."

"Right." I smile. "Steve can help you out."

I love that he remembers my appliance names. There were moments I'm not sure Alastair remembered *my* name, like that time he called me Bridget. That was my first clue something wasn't right in our relationship.

I glance out the window. The snow is falling harder, the toppled tree's branches sagging under the weight of the sparkly blanket of white. I wonder if we should go clear off the cars. Or shovel the roof to prevent ice dams. Or—

"Does your family still live around California?" I ask.

He nods, and I wait for the flash of wariness. For him to divert the question back to me. "All of them," he answers slowly. "My siblings, my parents. Even my grandma who's still alive." He smiles, and there's a flash of vulnerability in his eyes. "Mustard grandma. We're all within a ten-mile radius of each other."

"Wow." Talk about family closeness. "Do any of your siblings do set design?"

Gabe blinks. "What?"

"With you. I wasn't sure if it was a family business or—"

"Oh. Yeah. I guess we're all sort of in the business." He stands up fast, nearly knocking over his chair. "More coffee?"

"I'm good, thanks." I polish off the last bite of eggs and stand up to wash my plate, but Gabe beats me to it.

"I've got it." He takes the plate from my hands and sets to work scrubbing the pan and all the utensils in the sink. "You can dry."

"Deal."

We chat as we tidy up, glancing out the window every now and then to watch the snow piling up. I check my phone once in case there's a signal, but nope. "I wonder if they're getting this much snow back in Bend?" I ask.

"Could be." Gabe's eyes scan the massive drifts piling up at the edge of the porch. "It's sure beautiful."

"It is, isn't it?" Maybe I should stop worrying about getting out or getting home or getting busy shoveling. So what if we're stuck here for a day or two? It's not like Gabe is lousy company. Quite the opposite.

The thought of being all alone with him sends a shiver down my arms that's not entirely unpleasant. It should be. I'm doing it again, getting wrapped up in the idea of a sexy, smart, attractive guy without really knowing him at all. Taking a deep breath, I order myself to get a grip.

"What's that about?" he asks.

"What?"

He smiles. "You looked at me for a second like you thought about grabbing that butcher knife behind you and driving it into my spleen."

I laugh in spite of myself. "I'm really not that violent," I assure him. "I'm the one who should be afraid of you."

His eyes darken. Just a little, barely enough to register. But we're standing close together, so I see it.

"Why do you say that?" he asks softly.

Heat floods my body, but it's not a rush of danger. It's warmth from his closeness, from the electricity in his eyes. I try to remember what he just asked me. "I said I *should* be afraid of you," I answer. "I'm not, though."

"Why should you?"

I hesitate. How much should I share? "I just got out of a pretty bad relationship. I'm in kind of a vulnerable place."

The words sound raw and silly, and I instantly want to take them back. For crying out loud, I just implied he's liable to pounce on me.

But Gabe just smiles. "I won't pretend I'm not attracted to you," he says. "I think that's kind of obvious."

A flush creeps into my cheeks, and I force myself to hold it together. "You're also...not hideous."

He laughs and reaches for my hand. "Look, I won't claim to be a good guy. I'm about the furthest thing in the world from a good guy, but I can promise you one thing."

"What?" I ask, even though I'm dying to ask about the rest of that. Why doesn't he think he's a good guy?

"I promise I won't take advantage of you," he says. "I won't pressure you to do anything you don't want to do, and I won't ask you questions you don't want to answer. If anything gets physical between us, I will stop the instant you say stop. I won't promise anything I can't promise, but I will treat you with respect and kindness and honor."

All of that sounds amazing. His words, the sincerity in his eyes, all of it. They're exactly the words I wished Alastair would have said to me, the intention I wish he'd set.

But it's because of Alastair that I hear what's missing.

I won't lie to you

I'll let you in.

I'll be truthful about who I am and what I stand for.

It's dumb, because who says that? No one, not within twenty-four hours of knowing someone. Not while holding hands with a virtual stranger when you're trapped in a remote cabin.

Even so, I force myself to push my guard up. To acknowledge the good in what he said while steeling my heart against what wasn't said. "Thank you," I tell him. "I can promise you all the same. Kindness and respect and honor—I'm down with that."

He smiles, and all the uncertainty vanishes from his eyes. "And fresh-brewed coffee. But not ice cream."

"Can't have it all." I smile, grateful he's still touching me. That we're connecting on this level. And deep down, grateful we're stuck here with this time together.

"There's one more thing," he says.

"What's that?"

He grins and everything inside me goes molten and floods straight to my girl parts. "I promise to make you the best damn blanket fort you've ever seen."

I squeeze his hands and smile up into those brown eyes, hopeful I can hold on to my heart. "Deal."

CHAPTER 5

"*T*here." I pull one last clothespin out of my pocket and hand it to her. "Just tack up that corner and I think we're done."

Gretchen stares at me with a look I'm hoping is awe. It's either that or she's realized she's trapped in a cabin with a grown man who builds blanket forts.

Which is true, but I'm hoping that's a good thing.

"This is incredible." She pinches the clothespin into place, then sits back on her heels to admire the finished structure. Quilts swoop above us like magic carpets in flight. The floor is lined with couch cushions and another stash of blankets we unearthed from a closet beside the bathroom. There's even a string of Christmas lights Gretchen found in her car.

As she studies my handiwork, I study her. She's got her hair tied up again in one of those loopy topknots, which makes my fingers itch to touch it. The flannel overshirt is gone, leaving her in jeans and a white T-shirt I'm positive isn't meant to be sexy, but is hands down the most mouthwatering piece of clothing I've ever seen. Her cheeks are flushed, or maybe that's the Christmas lights flickering from green to red. When they go blue, her sea glass eyes become lit from within, and my heart balls up tight in my chest.

She turns and smiles at me, and the rest of my insides follow suit. Even my spleen clenches like a warm fist. "You were right," she says. "This puts my childhood blanket forts to shame."

"No shame here." I grin and dump a bag of Cheetos in a bowl, then set it on the shelf I made from a tray and two hunks of firewood. "It's a snow day. No feeling guilty about your dissertation or how we should be out shoveling. Everyone deserves a play day."

She closes her eyes and blows out a sharp breath, making wisps of hair flutter around her face. "I can't remember the last time I had one."

"Maybe getting stuck here isn't such a bad thing."

"Maybe." She smiles and flops onto her back on the nest of pillows. It's all I can do not to stare at her breasts moving under that T-shirt. I start to look away, but she speaks again. "Thank you for this, Gabe. It really is amazing." Her eyes twinkle as they sweep over the ceiling. "Seriously the coolest blanket fort ever."

"It's my proudest achievement." I'm only half joking as I shove past the voices in my head, reminding me of the litany of career achievements listed on my Wikipedia page.

What would it be like to leave all of that behind?

"Root beer?" I fish a hand into the mixing bowl I've filled with fresh snow and pluck out a can of A&W. Gretchen accepts it with a grin.

"Thank you." She rolls to her side and pops the top, throat moving as she swallows.

I take a sip of my own, hoping to cool my libido. She's getting over a breakup, and I'm hardly in a position to start anything romantic. We're friends, that's all. Friends trapped together in a snowy cabin. We can do this.

I stretch out beside her, careful to keep some distance between us. I heard what she said about feeling vulnerable. About reeling from a bad split. God knows I'm not in a place to go starting anything either.

Still, I can't help feeling drawn to her. Can't help noticing the click of electricity as my elbow grazes hers. "I'm glad you had all that laundry stuff in your car," I tell her. "The clothespins were handy."

"And the lava lamp." She reaches over and switches it on, giggling. "For the record, it was a gag gift. I wasn't even planning to keep it."

"I'm glad you did." I'm glad about a lot of things, starting with the fact that we're both here. I know it's nuts. I know I should be out shoveling or chopping wood or training courier pigeons to get a message to the outside world. But is there really a rush?

Gretchen takes another sip of root beer. "I didn't realize how much pressure I've been putting on myself," she says softly. "This dissertation's been dragging, so I tell myself I just need to work harder. To dig in deeper."

"And maybe what you really needed was a break?"

"Yeah." She smiles. "Maybe so. I'm not always awesome at knowing what I need."

My gut clenches at her words, and I'm not sure if it's another warning or if I'm reading too much into it. "So you're researching the foxes, plus your dissertation, plus you mentioned volunteering?"

"Yeah." Her expression's mildly sheepish. "Plus, I'm teaching a full load of classes." She turns her face to look up at the quilts that make our ceiling. "I was doing fine handling it all until the breakup." She shrugs, offering a weak smile. "I guess I'm still finding my feet. Finding the right balance between school stuff and personal."

There's something she's not saying. Something that just made her forehead crease, her eyes dim just a little. It's not my place to push, but I wonder if she'd feel better unburdening herself.

"I'm obviously not a college grad," I offer. "But from where I stand, you're doing a great job balancing things."

She laughs and sets her root beer on the shelf. "You're lying down, so I'm not sure whether to believe you."

My chest tightens, which is dumb. It's just an expression, not an indication she knows I'm an asshole liar. When she sits up, I'm half afraid she's leaving. "Time to color," she says. "Ready to find your creative muse?"

I roll onto my stomach to grab the Crayola box she hands me. "This is really a thing at the career counseling center?"

"Sort of." She flips open the crayon box and surveys the 64-pack with built-in sharpener. "We have coloring books instead of magazines in the waiting area. It's supposed to stimulate creativity."

I stare down at the book she's laid on the pillow between us. The cover is a cheerful kaleidoscope of bright flowers and swirls, with a happy little bird swooping across the top.

The Sweary Coloring Book for Adults.

"Your family's Christmas presents beat the hell out of mine," I say as she flips it open.

She laughs and flips the page. "This one was from Lily," she says. "She got one for Bree as a baby shower gift called *Mommy's Fucking Tired.*"

"Impressive." I flip through the pages, admiring the flourishes of leaves and flowers and frolicking puppies. "*Cocklump,*" I read off. "*Bullshit* is a nice one with those little bunnies."

Gretchen turns another page. "I like the hearts and kitties for *Fuckwit.*"

"*Whorebag* looks like it requires more artistic talent than I have."

"Same with *Twatwaffle.*" Gretchen frowns. "Is that a hedgehog on the *Clusterfuck* page?"

I peer at the black and white image. "Either that or an aardvark."

Gretchen flips back to the beginning. "How about *Cum dumpster*? You can work on one end and I'll do the other."

"Deal."

She turns the book sideways and presses the heel of her hand along the spine to flatten it open. I select a green crayon before grabbing the bowl of Cheetos off the shelf and offering it to Gretchen.

She waves it off. "Pass. I'm more of a sweet tooth snacker."

"Sorry about Sarah." I take a handful of Cheetos and set the bowl back on the shelf. "You going to survive without ice cream?"

"Maybe." She's using a purple crayon to outline the edge of the R at the end of *dumpster*, and I get mesmerized watching her long, graceful fingers.

"I brought Oreos, but I'll need to ration those," she says. "And I might have to take straight shots of the Hershey's syrup that was supposed to go on the ice cream."

I finish coloring the leaves around the edge of the C, then reach for the red crayon. "I might need you to give me the signs of sugar withdrawal and any first aid required."

"I'll draw you some instructions."

We color in silence for a bit, pages lit by the twinkling Christmas lights and the glow of the lava lamp. A log rolls over in the woodstove behind us, and I remind myself to stoke the fire soon.

But for now, I just enjoy the warmth of Gretchen stretched out beside me on the cushions, the sweet scent of her hair. I could get used to this.

"Tell me something, Gabe."

The seriousness of her tone sends a ripple of panic down my spine.

She knows.

She knows who I am and what I've done.

"What's that?" I manage to keep my voice light, despite the tension crackling up my spine.

"What's your last name?"

That's it. She suspects something. Maybe she googled before leaving town.

I glance at her, expecting to see those blue eyes boring into mine. But she's focused on the page in front of her, coloring like this isn't the single most crucial question she's asked me.

"Judson," I say softly. "My last name is Judson."

I could stop there. I should stop there.

But part of me wants her to know more. Know the whole me. "Actually, my first name isn't Gabe. It's Gable."

Something in my voice must catch her attention because she looks up from the page.

There's no trace of suspicion in her eyes. "Gable Judson." She says it with a lilt that's almost musical. It's so different from how TV announcers say my name that I almost don't recognize it as my own.

"Gable Judson," she repeats, smiling. "I get it."

I force myself to hold her gaze. Not to look away, though I urgently want to. "What do you get?"

"You said your parents are movie buffs, and you've got Lana and Lauren and Marilyn," she says. "So you must be Gable after Clark Gable."

My breath comes out in a slow leak. "Yeah," I murmur. "That's right."

"I've never seen a Clark Gable movie." She goes back to coloring, blue crayon tracing the edges of the P. "How about your brothers?"

I lick my lips, waiting for the other shoe to drop. For some of this to ring a bell. My whole family's been spread across headlines for generations. "Dean," I say slowly. "That's my older brother. And Cooper's younger."

She frowns, replacing the blue crayon in the box before selecting yellow. "Gary Cooper, right? From the song 'Puttin' on the Ritz.'"

"Right." I can't believe none of this is ringing a bell. *Cooper Judson. Dean Judson. Lauren Judson.* Our names have blazed across TV screens since we were babies.

But Gretchen keeps coloring, not alarmed in the least. "Do you prefer Gabe or Gable?"

I hold my breath. Hundreds of times, I've corrected reporters. *It's Gable, not Gabe.*

"Gabe," I tell her. "I like how you say my name."

She smiles and blows the hair off her forehead. "It's a fun name to say. *Gabe.* So strong and unassuming."

My heart balls up tight again. God, I could love this woman. *She doesn't even know you. Not the asshole you really are.*

"I like the name Gretchen, too. Gretchen—"

"Laslo," she supplies. "It's Hungarian."

"That's a nice name," I tell her. "I worked with a guy with the last name Laslo last year."

"Yeah? Was he a set builder, too?"

He wasn't. Not even close. He was a spoiled actor with overbleached teeth and a steroid habit.

But what's one more white lie?

"Yes." I hate myself instantly. More, I mean. "Actually, I'm thinking of leaving California." That's true. At least I can give her some shreds of the real me.

Gretchen looks up and cocks her head. "Where would you go?"

"I'm not sure. Just needing a change of scenery, you know? Some sort of major life change."

"I do know." She smiles and keeps shading the body of the puppy poised on the edge of the M. "I also know geographic cures aren't usually the solution to problems that aren't geographic in nature."

"What do you mean?"

She shrugs. "If your problem is that lava keeps sweeping through your living room, moving to a city without an active volcano would be a geographic cure. But if your problem is that you fall for the wrong kind of guy—hypothetically speaking—" She pauses, smiling to let me know it's not hypothetical. "—Or if you have a drug problem or something, moving to a new city won't solve it."

I let out a slow breath, grateful to be understood even if she doesn't know all the details. "Your problems just follow, you mean."

"Exactly."

She's right, of course. But I can't help thinking at least some of my problem *is* geographic. I wish I could tell her. I wish I could explain the whole, horrible mess.

But then she'd stop looking at me with that bright, brilliant smile, and I couldn't bear it. I just couldn't.

Gretchen tucks the yellow crayon in the box and reaches for a pink one. She's shading a flower, crafting beautiful swirls of color and texture. Once upon a time, I thought I was making something beautiful. How could I have known it would all turn to shit?

The silence stretches out, but it's not awkward. It's nice, actually. I imagine the snow muffling all sound, cushioning the sharp edges of the world outside. It's just the two of us here in this quilt-lined fort, breathing the warmth of cedar-tinged air.

It's the first time I've felt peaceful in—God, how long?

Gretchen shifts beside me. I glance over to see she's nibbling the edge of her lip.

"You okay?" I ask.

"Yeah. I just—" she takes a shaky breath and meets my eyes, the sharp blue piercing straight through me. "Can I confess something, Gabe?"

The air between us thickens. Whatever she's about to say means something. "You can tell me anything."

I'm surprised to see tears fill her eyes. She blinks them back and takes another breath. "I've never told anyone this," she says.

"But there's something about you—about this place—" She laughs and shakes her head. "This is coming out wrong."

"No, I know what you mean." I glance around at the blanket walls. "It's like our own little confession booth."

Her eyes brighten just a little. "Exactly." Another deep breath. "Anyway, I feel like I need to say it out loud at least once."

I nod, gripping my crayon tighter. "Whatever it is, I won't judge."

Her tiny ghost smile is gone in an instant. There's a stiffness in her shoulders that wasn't there before. When she speaks, her voice is barely a whisper. "I had an affair with a married man."

I force myself not to react. Not to judge. Not to ask questions. Just to let her speak.

But I do put a hand on hers, and that's enough to keep her talking. "I didn't know he was married," she says. "That's no excuse, but I wouldn't have gotten involved with him if I'd had any idea."

"You didn't know him well?"

Her laugh is sharp and bitter, not really a laugh at all. "We taught together for months. He was a professor in my department. We had parking spots next to each other, for crying out loud. I *should* have known."

I try to wrap my head around what she's telling me. Why these details matter. "You thought you knew him," I guess. "But it turned out you didn't."

Pain creases her forehead "I should have known," she says again. "I should have asked questions or googled him or driven past his house like any self-respecting stalker."

"But you trusted him."

"Yeah." She says it like it's the worst thing she's confessed so far. "He was older and more accomplished, and when he referred to his ex-wife, I didn't question if she really was an ex."

Clearly, she wasn't. And clearly this is something that's been tearing Gretchen apart. "How long did he fool you?"

She winces, making me regret my clumsy phrasing. I try again before she can respond. "How long did the lying rat bastard behave like a scheming piece of shit before you nailed his balls to the wall?"

Gretchen shakes her head and looks down at the page. "Two months." The words are a whisper, her eyes filled with guilt. "Two months before he called me by the wrong name, and I started asking questions. Even then, I believed him. I believed when he said they'd been separated for ages. That divorce paper-work was hung up in court, and they hadn't lived under the same roof in years."

"And the truth?"

"The truth." She shakes her head with a bitter little laugh. "The truth is that he'd fuck me after class and then go home to dinner with his wife and daughter."

"Jesus." I hate him. I hate him so much for lying to her. For making her feel like this. I curl my fingers around hers, willing her to believe me. "Gretchen, it wasn't your fault."

"No?" There's a cornered animal wildness in her eyes. "I'm a research scientist. I'm supposed to be inquisitive and curious and hungry for information. Why didn't I google him? Why didn't I question everything he told me? Why didn't I dig into his background?"

"Because you're a kind, honest, trusting soul." Even as I say it, the words ring hollow. I'm not exactly being straight with her myself.

She shakes her head slowly, tears glittering in her eyes. "I should have known," she says. "It's not just on him. It takes two to cheat, and I should have asked more questions. I should have—"

"Stop." I'm squeezing her hand now, willing her to hear me. "You can't make this your fault. There's only one person to blame here, and it isn't you."

She stares like she doesn't believe me, as the words echo in my head. How many times has my brother said this to me? Or my agent? Or—

"Gretchen, you have to believe me." She has to, because maybe it's the only way I can start believing it myself. "You're not the bad guy here. You're a sweet, generous, trusting person who got screwed by a guy who is none of those things."

I know she doesn't believe me, but she's looking me in the eye. Watching me like she wants to believe what I'm saying.

Maybe this is it. My segue to telling her my own big secret. My chance to come clean, to unburden myself to the most kind-hearted woman I've met.

I open my mouth to do it. To spit the words out like shrapnel. To put it out there so there are no secrets between us.

But I'm a big, fat chicken.

I choke. I fucking choke.

"Wait here." I let go of her hand and scramble to my knees to back out of the blanket fort. "I have an idea."

CHAPTER 6

GRETCHEN

$\mathcal{I}$'m trying not to freak out. I confess my worst secret to a good-looking guy—a guy I've kissed *twice*—and he disappears?

Granted, he can't go far. Not with a tree in our path and a blizzard raging outside. And he did say all sorts of kind, understanding things that I know aren't true, but I appreciate him saying them anyway.

So where did he go? And why do I want so badly for him to assure me I'm not a total screwup? Even if I'm not ready to believe that myself, I need to know he believes it.

The front door of the cabin bangs open, and I poke my head out of the blanket fort to see him striding toward the kitchen. In his hand is a big red mixing bowl.

"Not yet," is all he says as he shields the bowl from my view.

"Can I help with—"

"Nope, I'm good." He grins and waves me back into the fort. "It's a surprise. I'll bring it to you in just a second."

"Oh. Okay." I slip back under the quilts as a trickle of hopeful giddiness rinses away a bit of my guilt. Not all of it, of course. But maybe Gabe doesn't think I'm a jerk?

There's some banging from the kitchen, and the sound of him rummaging around in the fridge. Is he chopping something?

Then footsteps drum across the wood floors. "It's not perfect," he calls as the footsteps draw closer. "But it's pretty damn good."

He peels open the door of the blanket fort and crawls inside. The grin on his face melts my heart, and the Christmas lights brighten the amber flecks in his eyes. He smells like pinesap and woodsmoke and—

"Mint?" I blink at the bowl cradled in his arms. "Did you make something with mint?"

He sets the bowl in front of me like an offering, then hands me a spoon. "Fresh snow, caught right as it was falling from the sky so there's no risk a bear peed on it."

"Eew." I study the bowl, which is filled with a slushy mix drizzled in brown goo. It looks weird but smells promising. "Thank you?"

He laughs and whips out a second spoon. "I brought some peppermint schnapps, so I mixed that with the snow and a little milk, plus sugar and a chocolate bar I chopped up. Oh, and some of your Hershey's syrup."

"Oh my God." I throw my arms around his neck, nearly knocking over the bowl. "You made me mint chocolate chip ice cream?"

He laughs into my hair, arms sliding around my waist as he pulls me to him. "Yeah. You seemed like you could use a pick-me-up."

"This is amazing, Gable."

He stiffens in my arms, and I realize I've used his full name. An odd slip, since I only think of him as Gabe. He relaxes quickly, but I draw back anyway and cup his cheek in my palm. "Thank you, Gabe. This is the nicest thing anyone's done for me in a long time."

He grins and waves his spoon like a conductor's baton. "Dig in."

I do and, oh man, it's delicious. "Wow." I smack my lips, savoring the icy blend of sugar, mint, and chocolate with just a hint of boozy sweetness. "Watch out, Ben and Jerry. This is awesome."

"You like it?" He takes a spoonful for himself and grins. "I'm not a huge ice cream eater, but this seems pretty close."

"It might be even better," I tell him. "Very fresh."

There's the tiniest hint of pine, and I can't tell if it's in the snow or in Gabe's hair. Our spoons clink together as we go in at the same time. We both laugh, then keep scooping it up until the bowl is empty.

"How much schnapps was in there?" I ask.

"Maybe a tablespoon or so. Why?"

I meet his eyes, marveling at how close I feel to this guy I've known less than twenty-four hours. With less than a tablespoon of schnapps between us, I know it's not the booze, so it must be something else.

It must be Gabe.

I smile and set my spoon in the bowl. "I'm feeling warm and glowy. And it's apparently not the schnapps."

He smiles back, nesting his spoon in mine and setting the bowl on the shelf. "What is it?"

Happiness.

Gratitude.

Lust.

I don't say any of those things, though they're all true. His eyes stay fixed on mine, and I can tell he's thinking it, too. That we're trapped in a mountain cabin with plenty of food and firewood and all the privacy in the world. Why not have this time together? Just for a little while, what's the harm in giving in to what we both want?

You know the harm. You know exactly.

But I've stopped listening to that voice in my head. Gabe's

leaning in, and I'm moving to meet him, and there's nothing either of us can do to stop the force of us colliding.

The instant our lips touch, it feels like coming home. There's a certainty in his embrace, a softness I sink into like my feather duvet. He tastes like mint and desire and everything I've wanted from the moment I laid eyes on him.

Gabe slides his fingers into my hair, and I whimper as he deepens the kiss. My arms go around his waist by instinct, and I press my body to his. He's hard in all the right places, hot and solid against my softness.

God, he feels good.

"Gretchen." Breaking the kiss, he drops his lips to my throat. I tip my head back, digging my nails into his back to keep myself anchored. I know I should be careful. I know I've let passion sweep me away before.

But this feels like more than that. He's seen my ugliest underbelly and still wants me. I know him in a way I never knew Alastair.

His kisses travel across my collarbone, and I hold on tight. One of his hands slides under the hem of my T-shirt, then up again to cover my breast. I groan into his mouth.

"Don't stop, Gabe."

His thumb strokes my nipple, and I drop my hands to his ass to pull him tighter against me. I can feel the hard length of him behind warm denim, and a surge of need flares through me.

I want him.

"You taste so good." He's got my shirt up now, kissing my belly, my waist, my breast through the lace of my bra. His fingers slide up to work the clasp, and I sigh with pleasure as he sets me free.

Drawing back, I grab the hem of my shirt and pull the whole thing over my head. T-shirt, bra, all of it, so I'm stripped to the waist in the flicker of Christmas lights.

Gabe blinks. "You're so beautiful."

I laugh and pull him close. "Kiss me again."

He does, and it's glorious. How is it possible this keeps getting better each time? I don't know, and I give up trying to figure it out and just lose myself in the heat of his mouth, the roughness of his beard, the pressure of his hand on my breast.

Breaking the kiss again, he lays me back on the nest of quilts. I expect him to join me, but he sits there looking down at me. "God, Gretchen." He shakes his head in wonder, and I almost giggle. "I can't believe how perfect you are."

"Shut up." I laugh because I've just made this awkward, but also because I'm in awe. How could he think that?

As his mouth drops to my breast, all thinking flies out the window. I bury my fingers in his hair as his tongue circles my nipple, teasing and stroking and driving me insane.

"Gabe." I groan and close my eyes. "That's so good."

He moves to the other breast, taking his time. His kisses are slow and delicious and filled with heat. I know I should savor it, should seize the chance to go slowly.

But I want him so badly. I fumble for the front of his jeans and stroke the hardness there. He groans and presses into my hand. I open my eyes and find the tab of his zipper.

I start to tug, and everything goes black.

"What the—" I blink in the darkness as Gabe's mouth stills on my breast. "What just happened?"

My lust-fogged brain is grappling with the connection between Gabe's zipper and the lights. Luckily, he's slightly more lucid than I am. "Power's out," he says.

"Oh." No more Christmas lights. No lava lamp. No—

"Crap." I sit up fast, bumping my head on the shelf that holds the bowls. "Our food."

I can't see his face in the dark, but I hear him groan. "It should be good for a few hours, right?"

I bite my lip, as reluctant to stop as he is. "Do we really want to risk it? We don't know how long we'll be stranded, and with the perishable food—"

"No, you're right." He sighs as I fumble in the dark for my bra and wriggle it on.

"How many coolers do you have?"

"Two," he says. "You?"

"Same. We can fill them with snow and keep them outside for now."

"Good thinking."

Talk about miracles. Thinking clearly with a hot guy stripping me naked is not a skill I normally possess. Does this count as self-improvement?

Or maybe it's just Gabe. Maybe I'm different with him.

Pulling my shirt on, I follow him out the door of the blanket fort. There's still plenty of daylight, so we move quickly across the cabin. Even though I'm disappointed to have our hookup halted, I'm grateful we're on the same page. Survival comes first, even in the face of lust.

We work together assembling our coolers on the porch and filling them with fresh snow. Then we start clearing the fridge. Gabe hands me a package of bacon and some ground beef. "I suppose it's best not to take a risk with this stuff."

"Technically, it would have been okay for four hours." I shift the food into the crook of my arm and grab a gallon of milk. "That's how long the USDA says a fridge will stay cold in a power outage."

Gabe lifts both brows. "We could have accomplished a lot in four hours."

Heat rushes my cheeks as my imagination goes wild. He's not wrong, and I can't stop picturing it. He must read that in my eyes, because he kisses my cheek and grabs an armload of yogurt and juice. "But you're right, this is smarter. How'd you know that about the USDA?"

"Research." I trudge back to the porch with Gabe close

behind. "I did a paper on disaster preparedness back in undergrad."

He laughs as I pry the top off the first cooler and start loading things inside. "No wonder I didn't like college," he says. "I don't remember learning cool stuff like that when I was in school."

"That's right, I forgot I said I'd help you with a career quiz."

See? This is what happens when my libido takes over. One minute I'm a goal-oriented professional, the next I'm stripping off my bra in a blanket fort.

Maybe I should slow things down. I wipe my hands on my jeans and watch as Gabe loads the last of our perishables in the cooler. "If you want, we could do that now."

He blinks at me. "A career quiz?"

I open my mouth to explain. To tell him I want to slow things down just a bit.

But he somehow reads my mind. "I think that's great." He smiles and slides an arm around me, planting a kiss on my temple. "The snow's not stopping, so we've got plenty of time."

Relief washes through me. That he understands, that he's not pushing. I like Gabe, I do. But I want to be smart this time. Not throw myself at the first guy to grope me since Alastair.

I flash him a grin as I head back in the cabin. "Great. Let me see what I can find on my laptop."

"You do that, and I'll make lunch." He glances toward the kitchen, which is thankfully anchored by a gas-powered stove. "How's beef stew and apple slices?"

"Sounds like the quintessential snow day meal."

As Gabe busies himself in the kitchen, I settle at the table and boot up my laptop. Out of habit, I try to check my email, but there's clearly no signal. It's a weird feeling, but freeing. I've never been this cut off from the outside world.

It doesn't take long to locate the file filled with career questionnaires. As Gabe sets a bowl of stew next to me, I read off the first question.

"Gender—male or female?" I bite my lip and tick the correct box. "Um, male. Definitely. Very."

Gabe laughs and pushes a plate of apple slices between us. "You sure about that?"

"Pretty positive."

"Thanks for the vote of confidence." He bites off a piece of apple. "I'm already nailing this quiz."

And would likely be nailing me if the power hadn't gone out. I scroll down, intent on keeping us on neutral turf.

"This next set of questions requires you to pick between strongly agree, agree, disagree, or strongly disagree," I say. "Ready?"

"Lay it on me." He blows on a spoonful of stew, and I get distracted looking at his mouth.

"Question two." I take a bite of apple slice. *"Being around people gives me energy."*

"Hell, no."

I laugh and tick the box on the far right. "That wasn't one of the choices, but we'll go with 'strongly disagree.'"

"Fair enough." He scoops up more stew as I stir mine around and read the next question. *"I spend my spare time socializing, attending parties, and interacting with others."*

I glance up to see frown lines etching the space between his brows. "In my current life, or what I wish my life could be like?"

"Let's say your ideal world."

"Disagree," he says. "Maybe strongly."

I keep going, though I'm curious how much of his social interaction involves other women. Wait—

"You're not married, are you?" I stare into his eyes, willing him to be honest.

"What?" Gabe drops the apple slice he's holding. "Of course not. I'd never do that to you. Or to any woman."

"Right. Sorry."

He slides a hand over mine and squeezes. "Don't apologize. I understand why you're asking, and the answer's no. I'm not married or dating anyone. I promise."

Light sparks off the amber flecks in his eyes, and I remind myself not to fall for him. Or launch myself into his lap.

"I believe you," I tell him. "I do. I trust you to be honest with me."

Something twitches in his jaw. A muscle tick, or did he just clench? He stops before I can figure it out.

"What's next?" he asks.

There's a split second where I think he means us. Will we date after all this is over? Will we resume what got started in the blanket fort?

"The quiz," I say, forcing my eyes back to the questionnaire. "Okay, the next set of questions are behavioral. They're meant to test creativity and aptitude for outside-the-box thinking."

Gabe looks dubious. "Here's hoping the half-tablespoon of schnapps hasn't dulled my senses."

I know he's kidding, but I am kind of curious. I already know Gabe's smart, but I'm eager to see his brain in action. "Okay, *you can either ride an elephant or a giraffe. Which would you choose, and describe the challenges and advantages of your commute.*"

Gabe doesn't miss a beat. "The giraffe's going to be more nimble in LA traffic, since it features superior height and sighting capability and a narrower turning radius," he says. "The elephant would perform better in snow and could easily maneuver the tree out of the path of the car."

"I see." I'm impressed he's given it this much thought. If he were in the career counseling center, I'd give him high marks for creative thinking. "So you choose the elephant?"

"Giraffe," he says, smiling. "I'm not in any hurry to leave here at the moment."

Something in my center goes melty, but I order myself to stay focused. I take a bite of stew and scroll down the page. "Let's move on to analytical questions." I scroll down the page, trying to find a good one. "Okay, *you encounter two guards, each blocking a door. One door leads to eternal doom, the other leads to endless ice cream.*"

I might have improvised that last part, but Gabe grins. "Are we talking chocolate chip mint, or plain old vanilla?"

"This has bearing on your answer?"

"Absolutely. I'd risk eternal damnation to bring you mint chocolate chip."

"You are ridiculously sweet." I ignore the melting of my heart and gesture to the screen. "May I continue with the question?"

"By all means."

I scan to find my place again. "*Two guards, two doors. One leads to the ice cream, one to eternal damnation. One of the guards only tells the truth, and the other is only capable of lying.* You with me so far?"

"Yep," he says. "Ice cream, damnation, a lying guard, and one who tells the truth."

"Right. *You can ask one guard a single question. Who do you pick and what do you ask in order to get to the ice cream?*"

I look up again and see he's puzzling away. He stares out the window, watching flakes fall as he considers the question.

While he's doing that, I consider Gabe. I love the play of light in his eyes. I love that he keeps nudging the apples closer to me, trying to make sure I get my fair share. I love that he's giving this question such careful thought.

"I'd choose one guard and ask, 'if I asked the *other* guard which door leads to ice cream, what would he tell me?' If I've picked the truth-telling guard, he's going to be honest when he tells me the other guy's going to point to the door with the damnation."

"Uh-huh," I say, impressed he figured it out this quickly. "And if you've asked the liar guard?"

"Obviously I won't know at the time he's the liar," he reasons. "But I give him the same question—'what would the *other* guard tell me if I ask which door has the ice cream?'—he has to lie and point to the door that leads to damnation. Either way, I know where the ice cream is."

"Damn." I look up from the laptop. "Most people don't figure it out that fast."

Gabe grins, and my insides go gooey. "Is this helping you figure out my future career?"

It's helping me figure out that Gabe Judson is clever, in addition to sexy and funny. God help me.

"Yes," I say honestly. "You'd be good at a career that requires spontaneous, creative thinking."

"Which would be what, exactly?"

I scroll down to find a partial list. "Architect. Floral designer. Art director. Glass blower. Web developer. There are at least a hundred options here. I can send it to you when I'm back to an internet connection."

Back to real life. Away from this sweet little utopia we're creating here. The thought makes me sad.

"What about shepherd?" he asks. "Or astronaut. I always thought I had a future as an astronaut."

I laugh and scrape up the last of the stew from my bowl. "That's just a preliminary list. Want to keep going?"

Gabe grabs another apple slice and nods. "I could go all night."

My panties melt on the spot. I tear my eyes off him, fighting to keep my brain out of the gutter as I scroll to one of the quizzes I haven't used before. Might as well learn something new.

"Let's do another question."

Gabe grins like he knows I just pictured him naked. "Let's."

"Okay, you have eight penises," I read. *"Seven of the penises weigh the same, and one weighs less."*

It occurs to me something's off about this question, but I forge ahead, determined to stay focused. *"You also have a judge's scale to weigh all the penises. Find the one that weighs less in three steps."*

I look up to see Gabe staring at me. "Is this a trick question?"

"Um." I glance back at the monitor, trying to find my place in the questionnaire. "I've actually never asked this one before. Hang on—"

"Because if I did have eight penises, I wouldn't care what any of them weighed," he says. "I'd be focused on finding underwear that fits. And figuring out how not to make a scene at public urinals. And being sure the woman I'm crazy about is comfortable with my genital deformity. That's you, by the way. Oh, and also, I'd be worried about riding a bike or—"

"Pennies!" I shout, jabbing a finger at the screen. "*Pennies*, not penises. I read the question wrong." Heat rushes to my cheeks as I do my best not to look at Gabe. And definitely not at Gabe's crotch.

Probably how you read the word wrong in the first place.

He squeezes my hand, still laughing. "Don't feel bad. Want me to tell you about the time I mispronounced the word 'pianist' in front of ten thousand people?"

"Ten thousand p—" I stop mid-question as my brain backs up and stalls on his earlier words. The romantic bit between between "public urinals" and "genital deformity."

I blink at him. "You're crazy about me?"

Gabe grins. "Very much so."

"I see." My cheeks are still hot, but for a different reason now. "Did you want to address the question with pennies instead of penises?"

He shrugs and releases my hand. "Might as well stick with penises, if that's what you have on your mind."

Oh, God. He's right; he's totally right. Blame it on our blanket fort groping. "Um, I don't—"

"Let's see," he says, leaning back in his chair. "To figure out which of the penises is lightest, I'd start by creating two groups of three penises each. Then I'd also have one group of two penises."

"You're creating quite the mental picture."

He quirks an eyebrow. "Can't stop thinking about it, huh?"

You have no idea.

"Continue," I prompt, waving a hand. "Two groups of three penises and one group of two."

"Right, so I start by putting the groups of three penises on the scale—one on each side. This is one of those old-fashioned hanging scales, right?"

"Correct." It's all I can do to keep a straight face right now. "It'll have to be a big scale to fit that many penises."

Gabe laughs and leans back, folding his hands behind his head. "Oh, I'm very adept at penis management."

My mouth goes dry, but I force myself to nod. "So what next?"

"Well, with a set of three penises on each side of the scale, I'll know right away whether the lightest penis is in one of those two groups. If they're equal, the light one is in the group of two."

"Very clever." Have I mentioned I love smart guys? And guys with broad chests and warm brown eyes and— "Okay, so let's say the two sets of three weigh the same." I'm struggling like hell to stay on topic. "What do you do with the two penises?"

"One on each side of the scale, of course," he says. "I've got my answer in two steps."

"And what if the first round goes differently?" I ask. "If one of those stacks of three is lighter. How do you know which penis is the light one?"

"Easy." The flash in his eyes tells me he's enjoying this way too much. "Pick two out of the three penises and put one on each side of the scale. If they're equal, the third penis is the light one. If they're not—bingo! There's my light penis."

"Light penis." I grin. "Is that like a light saber?"

Gabe clasps his hands over his chest and gasps. "Be still my heart. You know *Star Wars*?"

I laugh and shove my empty bowl aside. "I haven't been living in a cave. Everyone knows *Star Wars*."

He performs an elaborate sort of swoon, hands still clutching his chest. "Promise me when we get out of here, you'll let me take you on a movie date. It doesn't have to be *Star Wars*; it can be anything."

I bite my lip, considering the offer. "I did want to see *Finding Nemo*. I tried to watch it with Libby, but when Nemo's mom dies in the first five minutes—" I shrug, already feeling silly.

"You never watched the end of it?"

I shake my head. "It was too sad."

He studies my face, slow smile spreading over his. "You're fucking adorable, you know that?"

I laugh and tuck some loose hair behind my ear. "Anyway, I agree."

"To what?"

"A movie date. If the offer still stands?"

"Oh, it stands." He grins. "I'm already planning it. You. Me. A bucket of popcorn. An excuse to steal a kiss in the dark."

I glance around the cabin. There's still sunlight streaming through the windows, but it won't be long before the cabin's plunged into darkness. We've already gathered all the candles in the house, but the thought of being trapped in the dark with Gabe isn't as scary as it should be.

When I meet his eyes again, my stomach swirls like a chocolate/vanilla cone. "It's not stealing if I offer the kiss freely," I point out. "And it might be a while until we have access to movies."

His eyes don't leave my face, but they do flash with intrigue. "What are you suggesting?"

I lick my lips, knowing how much hinges on what I say next. How much things can change by falling casually into bed with someone I don't know.

But I *know* Gabe. There's something about forced togetherness, about having this much dedicated time together. I swear I feel closer to him than I do with colleagues I've known for months. It's like we've peeked inside each other's souls and discovered we both like what we see.

I push my laptop closed and stand up.

"Come on." My hand trembles only a little as I point to the blanket fort. "I know where there's a dark spot."

He looks at me with a question in his eyes. *Is this what I think it is?*

I nod at the same time he asks, "Are you sure?"

"Yeah. Yes, I am." I haven't been this sure of anything for a long time.

The smile that spreads over his face is warm and golden as honey. "A dress rehearsal?"

My heart pounds in my ears, but it's the good kind of pounding. The second best. "How about an undressed rehearsal?"

Before he can respond, I grab the hem of my T-shirt and pull it over my head. Then I hand it to him, heart thudding in my throat as Gabe gapes at me in wonder.

"Meet you in the fort," I tell him.

Then I turn and cross the room on shaky legs.

CHAPTER 7

GABLE

Oh my God.

My mouth goes dry as I watch Gretchen's bare back retreat across the room. Her skin is flawless, and the smile she throws over her shoulder turns my chest cavity into a simmering bowl of want. I look down and see I'm clutching her T-shirt so hard my knuckles are white.

Tell her.

The voice in my head is screaming it. Reminding me that before this goes further, she needs to know who I am and what I've done. I've had plenty of chances. She deserves the story.

But as I fold her shirt and lay it on the table, I can't seem to find my voice. I still can't find it as I follow her across the room, anticipation swelling like a lava-filled balloon in my chest. I'm three feet away, and I can already feel her.

She turns in the doorway of the blanket fort and smiles. My breath catches in my throat as I let my gaze sweep her shoulders, her breasts, her belly. A deep flush spreads over her cheeks, and I know self-consciousness is setting in.

"Gretchen." I reach for her, sliding my palms into the warm, bare curve of her waist. "You're so beautiful."

She laughs, but there's a note of uncertainty in it. "Thank you."

"No, thank you." I kiss the spot just below her ear, breathing her in. "Thank you for inviting me to dinner." I kiss her again, lower this time along the curve of her neck. "And for kissing me goodbye this morning instead of charging off into the blizzard."

If she hadn't, who knows where she'd have been when that tree fell?

And who knows where we'd be now?

I move lower, skimming my lips over her throat. "And thank you for taking off your shirt." She shivers as I plant one more kiss on the tender spot where her neck meets her shoulder. "And for whatever's about to happen between us."

She shivers again and draws back to meet my eyes. Her smile is warm as she squares her shoulders. "Look, I know we're both at weird places in our lives. And I know this can't mean anything. So why don't we just enjoy it for what it is?"

I shake my head, determined to be honest in this at least. "No." I skim my hands up her ribs, watching her shiver. "It means something to me. It means *everything*. That's the only way I'm doing this."

She holds my gaze with hers, studying me like she's trying to see into my soul. I want her to know she can believe me. Even if I haven't told her everything, this much is true. This isn't a fling for me.

"Yeah," she says softly. "It's more to me, too. I didn't mean it to be, but—"

"I know." I kiss her shoulder again, needing to memorize the sprinkle of freckles on pale skin. "Same."

So there it is. We're on the same page, at least as far as what comes next.

Same page? You haven't even given her the book, asshole.

I push aside the self-doubt and pull her into my arms, kissing her long and deep as her fingers twine in my hair. Her soft sigh of pleasure blows the dark thoughts into a far corner of my brain. There's time for truth-telling later. Right now, this is the only truth that matters.

It's Gretchen who kisses first this time, pulling me down so my mouth meets hers. We're slow at first, tentative, like we're both coming to terms with this new understanding.

That doesn't last long. Hunger takes over, and soon we're clawing at each other's clothes. Her bra goes first as she works the fly of my jeans. Neither of us breaks the kiss, not even to come up for air. We're fused together, each of us needing this as much as the other.

"God, Gretchen." I breathe the words against her throat, laying a path of kisses down her chest. Sinking to my knees, I worship her breasts, licking and sucking until she clutches my hair and cries out.

"Gabe." Her knees wobble, and I grip her waist to keep her upright. "Let's go inside. Please. I want to feel you."

I don't know if it's the urgency in her voice or the way she says my name, but my heart curls into a contented ball. I get to my feet, conscious of the shakiness of my legs.

"I've never wanted anyone this much." I squeeze her fingers, hoping she believes me. "Not ever."

It's the God's honest truth. One day when the rest of my truths are laid out, I hope she still believes this one.

Her smile sends a burst of sunlight straight to my soul. "Same." She catches my hand in hers and tugs. "Inside. Now."

I don't need to be asked again.

She ducks down to enter the cozy cave of blankets, and I follow behind, unable to keep my hands off her. Panties are the only scrap of clothing she has left, and I plan to remedy that soon.

Inside the fort is darker than it was before, the Christmas lights now just glass bulbs tipped with sunlight streaming through the window behind us. I leave the door flap open, needing to see her. To memorize every detail of her body.

Settling into the nest of blankets, she leans back on her elbows with blue eyes blazing. "I've never had sex in a blanket fort before."

"Me, neither." I kiss her, easing her back. "I mean, not with anyone besides myself."

She laughs and wraps her arms around my back. "Perv."

"I was a pre-teen boy," I say as I kiss my way down the middle of her chest. "Privacy's hard to find in a big family."

"I'll give you points for creativity." With a couple quick tugs, she's got my shirt off and goes to work on my pants. Sliding her hand into my boxer briefs, she grins and wraps her fingers snug around my shaft.

"Only the one penis." She grins and licks her lips. "I'm relieved."

I bust out laughing, drunk on the combination of lust and humor. There should be a law requiring more laughter in bed. It would make the world a better place. "Let me know if you want to weigh it."

Her laugh becomes a gasp as I hook my thumbs in the waist-band of her panties and drag them down her legs. She groans again as I kiss my way down her center, rolling until I slip between her thighs.

The instant my mouth finds her slick center, she cries out. "Gabe!" Fingers clutch my hair as she arches up against me. "Don't stop."

I didn't plan on it. She's so wet, so goddamn sweet. I could do this all night, worshiping her with my lips, my tongue, my fingers. I've wanted this from the first moment I saw her. Needed to feel her slick and warm around me, filling my senses the way she is now.

"Oh God." Her walls clench around my fingers, surprising me

with how fast she's reached her peak. I ride the wave with her, licking and sucking until she goes slack in my hands.

Then I pull her to me and wait for her breathing to slow, for her heart to stop thudding against my chest.

"Later." She presses her palms to my chest, breathless and grinning. "Snuggling can wait. I need you inside me now."

My dick practically sits up and begs, but I manage to hold it together. "We can arrange that."

"Thank God."

Her bluntness, the nakedness of her desire—it's an even bigger turn-on than her body. I fumble with my wallet, grateful I've got one condom tucked away. She helps roll it on, then pulls me between her thighs as I tip her onto her back.

I hesitate, holding myself at her opening with every ounce of self-control I possess as I look in her eyes to be sure she's still with me.

"Yes," she says, even though I didn't ask out loud. "Please, Gabe."

I ease in slowly, or at least I try to. She's got her legs wrapped tight around me, drawing me into her warm center. I drive in deeper than I mean to, but her gasp is pure pleasure.

"Yes," she says again, arching tight against me. "*Yes.*"

I struggle to keep control, to make this last. Her body surrounds me like we're made to fit together. Like the puzzle piece I've searched for my whole life is finally slipping into place.

Her blue eyes are wide and locked on my face. I've never been one for eye contact during sex, and a ripple of panic moves through me. But Gretchen smiles, and my tension dissolves. I can't look away. Can't pull back from the overwhelming joy of being seen, being truly *seen*, by someone like her.

She doesn't know you—

But she *does* know me. Maybe not the Gable Judson from the headlines. The Gable Judson who's spent his life in the spotlight.

But maybe that was never the real me.

"Gabe." She closes her eyes as I drive in deeper, hitting something that makes us both groan.

Her thighs grip me tighter, and I know she's getting close. "Oh, *yes*."

I can't believe how good she feels, how perfect this moment is. The soft brush of quilts, the smell of woodsmoke, the pure, naked intimacy of being together like this.

There's a roar in my head getting louder, and I fight it back. I need to make this last. I need to bring her there. I need—

"Oh, God, Gabe. *Now*."

The roar slips through my lips, and we cry out together. I drive in deep as she spasms around me, body arching like a bow. I can't tell where her screams end and mine begin, and I'm grateful we're the only humans for miles.

It's just us. Only us as we lose ourselves in each other's arms and the ripples of pleasure go on and on and on.

* * *

I DON'T KNOW how long we lie breathless in the fort, tangled together in quilts and the world's most amazing afterglow. I can't stop kissing her temple, her ear, the pulse fluttering in her throat. I can't stop breathing her in, marveling that salmon chowder and fallen trees and accidental gunpoint threats turned into the best sex of my life.

Gretchen slides an arm over my torso and angles herself up. She peers at me with a beam of sun spotlighting her eyes, hair spilling over my chest like silk.

"Tell me about being a set designer," she says.

There's a crashing sound in my ears, which might be reality clubbing me between the eyes. I draw in a slow breath. "What do you want to know?"

"I'm curious," she says. "If it's something you've done for a while and you're looking to get out of, maybe it would help to know what you've liked and disliked about the job."

This is my chance. I know I need to tell her. The words are on the tip of my tongue.

Actually, Gretchen...

"Set designers work with directors and producers and costume designers to come up with the sets used in film and TV." The words are stiff and flattened by self-loathing. "There's a lot of drawing up plans and building models, plus budgeting and visiting sites."

I close my eyes, unable to bear looking at her.

It wasn't technically a lie. She asked what a set designer does, and you told her.

That's no excuse.

"What about the hands-on stuff?" she asks. "The grunt labor of actually building the set."

"There's some of that, too," I tell her. "Especially on lower-budget productions."

"And do you like that?"

"Working with my hands?" I slide mine up her body, one palm tracing her shoulder blades while the other circles the small of her back. "Yeah. I like it a lot."

She laughs and traces a fingertip through my chest hair, playing an invisible game of connect the dots. "I imagine you watch a lot of TV and movies?"

"Yeah." God, this feels good. Not just Gretchen's skin, warm and smooth under my palms, but this moment. This pillow talk, the soft lull of conversation. It feels so...normal. So unlike my regular life.

I try to remember what we were talking about. Television? "Yeah, I watch a lot. Movies and TV both." Her breath fans warm across my chest, and I let my own breathing sync with hers. "It's partly to keep up on the industry. Partly just for pleasure."

"Pleasure, huh?" There's a teasing note in her voice and her touch as she circles a fingertip around my nipple. "Hope you're not feeling too deprived in that department."

I laugh and pull her closer, crushing her breasts against my chest. "If I packed any more pleasure into my life right now, I would probably die from it."

"Mmm, we wouldn't want that." She dots a kiss on my pec, then scatters a few more across my chest. "What are some of your favorite shows?"

I'm relaxing into her, savoring the feel of her body warm against mine. This conversation is probably fraught with land-mines, but part of me doesn't care. "*Stranger Things*," I murmur, skimming a palm down her ribs. "It's a TV show."

"What's it about?" She jerks in my arms, then sits up grinning. "Wait, no, don't tell me."

"What?"

She's grinning, and there's a lot of bouncing going on, so I miss part of what she's saying as she digs through the blankets. "...can help you stave off the television withdrawals."

When she pops back up, she's got her blue and white snowflake socks in her hands and a mischievous glint in her eyes. With sex-tousled hair and bare breasts bathed in filtered sunlight, she's the most beautiful woman I've ever seen.

Beautiful and a little deranged. "What's with the socks?" I ask.

"It's show biz, baby." Still grinning, she yanks one on each hand and jams a fist into the toe of each sock. Wriggling her fingers into position, she holds her hands up sock-puppet style.

"Hello there, Jim." Her left hand mouths the words as Gretchen does the goofiest voice I've ever heard "Between the following two things, which is stranger?"

It's the right hand's turn, and Gretchen pitches her voice lower. "Oh, you mean like *Stranger Things*, Bob?"

"Exactly! That's the show, Jim."

I laugh and roll onto my back, loving this version way more than the one on Netflix.

"Which is stranger," Gretchen repeats in her Bob voice. "Putting carrots in Jell-O salad, or people who wash down Doritos with Diet Coke?"

She maneuvers the Jim sock into a thoughtful pose, and I laugh again. "Definitely the carrots, Bob."

"Good point, good point." Gretchen wriggles the Bob puppet in apparent approval. "How about tube tops or the fact that there's no such thing as B batteries?"

I fold my hands behind my head, enjoying the show. "I never thought of that," I muse. "There's A batteries and C and D—"

"Do you hear something, Bob?" Gretchen turns both sock puppets to face me. "That sounds like a heckler."

Laughing, I pantomime zipping my lips shut.

The show goes on.

"Which is stranger?" Jim continues. "The fact that the US doesn't use the metric system, or the fact that an Echo Dot imitates human flatulence when you say, 'Alexa, make fart noises.'"

I crack up again, shaking my head. "That can't be real."

"It *is* real, Bob," Gretchen says through puppet Jim. "You'd know that if you had a gross older brother."

"True, true. Those are pretty strange as well." Bob looks pensive, or as pensive as a sock can look. "What about breasts?"

"What about breasts, Bob?"

"Is it stranger that men can walk around shirtless, or that women can cover up everything but their nipples, and it'll somehow be indecent?"

I roll to my side, enjoying the show too much to shut up. "That's an excellent point," I say. "Also, the puppeteer has the most beautiful breasts I've laid eyes on."

Gretchen smiles but doesn't break character. "Well, Jim—I'd say all of those things are pretty strange."

Bob nods as Gretchen moves her arm, giving me another glimpse of those perfect breasts.

She holds the puppets out to the sides and grins. "And that concludes today's episode of *Stranger Things*."

I break into applause as she contorts both puppets into a courtly bow. "Nailed it," I say, still clapping. "That's exactly what *Stranger Things* is about."

"Thank you." Gretchen takes a bow of her own, golden hair skimming her breasts. "How about movies? Give me a big hit to work with."

A knot forms in the center of my chest, but I push past it. My mother's favorite movie is the first one that comes to mind, so that's what I give her.

"*A Star is Born* is pretty cool," I admit, tracing a fingertip over Gretchen's bare knee. "The original from 1937 starred Janet Gaynor and Fredric March, but my favorite is the 1954 version with Judy Garland and James Mason."

Gretchen lowers the sock puppets and quirks an eyebrow. "Not the one with Lady Gaga?"

"Whoa, look who knows movies after all!"

She shrugs. "I sometimes catch the headlines, so I knew about that one. Can't say I have any idea what the movie's about." Grinning, she lifts the sock puppets again. "But Jim and Bob do."

I laugh as she spurs the puppets back into action. "Tell me, Bob, how is it that stars come to be born?"

"Well, Jim," she responds, making my heart melt with those adorable voices. "Stars are formed within clouds of dust and gas you'll find scattered throughout most galaxies."

She gives a low guffaw on behalf of Jim. "There's an awful lot of gas in my galaxy, Bob."

Gretchen rolls her eyes and leans close to whisper an aside. "Puppets—how crude."

"So hard to manage," I agree. "I do want to hear about the stars, though."

"Right." She lifts the socks again and slips back into puppet voices.

"We're talking about molecular clouds, Jim. Stay with me here."

"Right, right," the second puppet says. "So how does that become a star?"

"I'm glad you asked, Jim, since I've never had use for that undergrad astronomy course until now." Gretchen blows a lock of hair off her forehead. "Turbulence within those dust clouds form knots of matter with enough mass that the gas and dust collapse under their own gravitational attraction. When that happens, the material at the center heats up to form a star."

"Mmm, I like it when things heat up," she says on behalf of puppet Jim, then wiggles her brows at me. "Such a perv."

"I think I like Jim," I tell her. "But not as much as I like you."

"Thank you." She does another topless curtsey, lifting the puppets to do a bow of their own. "This ends tonight's production. Stay tuned for more entertainment."

"I like the sound of that." I slip my arms around her waist and pull her down to me, kissing her on the mouth. "Thank you for that."

"Don't mention it." She snuggles against me, one sock hand trailing over my bicep. "It's the least I could do after you made me ice cream."

"That was amazing." Another kiss, this one between her breasts. "*You're* amazing."

She strips off the socks, laughing as she rolls onto her back. "You're not so bad yourself."

I'm still laughing as I kiss my way down her center, tongue circling her belly button.

But the way I'm feeling is no laughing matter. I'm falling for Gretchen.

And there's not a damn thing I can do about it.

CHAPTER 8

GRETCHEN

The next forty-eight hours are a blur of snuggling and shoveling, sex and schoolwork. I'm grateful I had both a solar charger and a box of condoms in my glovebox, both of which needed to be thawed before use.

Though the power returns that first evening, we eat our meals by candlelight. We take turns keeping the fire going, watching through frosted windowpanes as the snow slows, then eventually stops falling.

On the morning of the third day, we wake to the sun blasting bright beams through the trees. I step out onto the porch, blowing on my hands as I survey the vast blanket of white in front of me, the ocean of blue above.

"Damn, that's beautiful." Gabe strolls onto the porch with two steaming mugs of coffee.

I look up and smile, accepting the mug he hands me. "It's always so pretty after a storm like that."

He grins and slips an arm around my waist. "I was talking about you."

"Goofball." I lift the mug to my lips. "Thanks for this."

"No problem. Figured you needed dissertation fuel."

"Actually, I'm thinking I'll head out."

"Out." He cocks his head. "Out where?"

"To town." I sweep a hand toward the road, which is still blocked by the fallen tree. "I've got my snowshoes, and the snow's had time to set up. Shouldn't take more than an hour, hour-and-a-half to make it to town and call for help."

Gabe frowns. "That doesn't sound safe."

"It's perfectly safe," I insist. "I snowshoed competitively in high school and college. I know how to pace myself, and there's no sign of more snow on the way."

Gabe's still frowning, one shoulder braced against the side of the cabin. "I'll come with you."

"That won't work," I remind him. "I've only got the one set of snowshoes. You'll be post-holing up to your crotch if you try to go without."

"I don't like this. What about bears or cougars or...or Sasquatch?"

"I have a gun," I point out. "And bear spray."

"Bear spray?" He quirks an eyebrow. "I guess I'm grateful you picked the gun that first morning."

Man, that seems like a lifetime ago. Crazy how much has happened since then. "I'll be fine," I tell him. "The next storm isn't supposed to move in 'til next week, so now's our chance to get someone out here to help with the road and the tree."

Even as I say it, I feel wistful. Something in Gabe's eyes tells me he feels the same about our time alone coming to an end. He shifts closer, slipping an arm around my waist.

"You mean we don't get to stay here forever?" he asks as he nuzzles my neck.

"Maybe not here." I choose my words carefully, not sure we're on the same page. "But I'm game for continuing this back in the real world."

Is it my imagination, or does he stiffen? It's only for an instant, then he goes back to nuzzling my neck. "I'm game."

"Yeah?" We haven't really talked about this.

"Definitely."

"Okay then." Part of me feels giddy. A smaller part—a tiny, minuscule corner—worries we haven't spent enough time talking about this. "Okay, so I'll get help." I groan as he massages my breast through the thick flannel shirt. "And once we're settled, we'll talk about what the future looks like."

"Deal." Gabe straightens and sighs. "You sure about leaving?"

"It's safe, I promise."

His brow furrows, but he almost looks convinced. "I guess it's easy to see where the road is. And we're not that far from town."

"I'm a pro." I grin and set my mug on the railing. "I'll call my brother from town and have him get someone out here with chainsaws and a plow truck. We'll be free by afternoon."

Gabe kisses me again, brown eyes searching mine. "What if I don't want to be free?"

"I can always tie you up," I tease. "I'll use the sock puppets if we can't find rope."

He laughs and hugs me tighter. I bury my face in his chest and wrap my arms around his waist, breathing him in. How is it possible to feel this close to someone I've known just a few days?

"All right," he says at last. "If you're not back in three hours, I'm setting out on foot to find you."

"Four hours." I draw back, planting a kiss on his jaw before turning to head inside for my gear. "I need time to find a signal and make calls, plus I'll want to restock some groceries." And condoms. A girl's gotta plan ahead.

Gabe follows me inside, supervising as I stuff supplies in my day pack. "Please be careful."

"I'm always careful." With my body, my heart, my well-being.

"Four hours," he says as he hands me a bag of trail mix. "I mean it, don't take any unnecessary risks."

"It's not risky," I assure him. "Just flat road from here to the highway."

He sighs and pulls me to him again. I feel his heart thudding through my parka, feel the heat of his body rising off his arms. When he draws back and looks deep in my eyes, I can see he wants to say something. To confess something, maybe.

I've seen this look countless times over the last couple days, but he always seems to stop himself. A ripple of nerves moves through me. I tense, waiting for the other shoe to drop. What's happening here?

Gabe looks deep into my eyes. I don't think he's breathing. "I love you."

I blink, pretty sure I've heard wrong. Or maybe it just slipped out. I wait for him to backtrack, to tell me he misspoke.

"I love you," he repeats, smiling a little. "I know it's dumb, but—"

"No way is that dumb." I set my pack down and lace my fingers through his. My heart thunders in my ears as I hear the words echoing through my brain.

I love you.

I love you.

He really just said that.

"I love you, too." I breathe the words like a prayer, dumbfounded by how fast this is happening. "I can't believe it, but it's true. I'm so glad."

"Me, too." He squeezes my fingers. "Best damn dinner invitation I ever accepted."

I laugh and stretch up to kiss him one more time. "Best outcome I've had from pulling a gun on someone."

"Come back soon," he says. "Then we'll figure out where we go from here."

"Deal." Grabbing my gear, I head out onto the porch to put on my snowshoes. He waves goodbye from the front door as I set out down the snow-covered road at a steady clip.

I think about his words all the way back to town. Not just the L-word, but the comment about where we go from here. My limbs burn with the first non-sexual exercise they've had in days, but my heart is warm for other reasons. I don't know what sort of future Gabe and I might have together, but I know I want one.

Is that what he meant about figuring out where we go from here? Maybe I'm naïve, but I can't help thinking he wants the same thing I do.

It's barely ten-thirty when I reach the highway. The asphalt's dotted with hunks of melting snow, and there's a berm of brownish slush on both sides. I sit down on a concrete barrier to take off my snowshoes and watch cars whiz past, wondering if I should flag one down. A glance at my watch tells me I've made good time, so I stuff the shoes in my pack and set out walking toward the grocery store.

I reach the parking lot in less than ten minutes, weaving through dirty piles of snow and the beeping, growling plow trucks. Slipping my phone out of my pocket, I use my teeth to pull off a glove. There's a picnic table near the store entrance, a throwback to sunnier days in this Central Oregon desert town. I park myself there and hit speed-dial for Jonathan.

My brother picks up on the first ring. "Gretchen. God, are you okay? I know you grew up in this crap, but I've been worried."

"I'm fine, I'm great." And grateful my brother knows me well enough not to send out a search party at the first sign of snow. "Actually, I'm pretty fantastic."

There's a long pause before he responds. "Why do I get the feeling this has nothing to do with your dissertation?"

Because cupid nabbed your ass a few months ago, big brother.

I don't say this out loud, but I can't hold back completely. "Um, well…I might not have been out there in the woods alone."

And I might have found creative ways to stay warm.

Jon gives a low whistle. "I knew you were seeing some guy from school, but I didn't realize he went with you."

Alastair? "How did you know about that?"

"Just a hunch," Jon says. "You never introduced us, so I figured it wasn't serious."

"Oh. Um, well, thank you for not going all aggro big brother and demanding to meet him."

He laughs, and the sound fills me with home. "Please. You're a smart, independent woman who makes good choices. You don't need me to barge in beating my chest like some caveman douchebag." There's a quick pause. "I will, though, if you need me to."

I close my eyes, unsure how we got going down this path. *You're a smart, independent woman who makes good choices.*

If he only knew the shame I've carried these last few months.

But that's not what this call is about. I open my eyes and try to steer the conversation back to present tense. "No, not the guy from the college," I tell him. "We broke up a while ago. This is actually a friend of James."

"Who is?"

"*Gabe.* The guy I've been snowed in with at the cabin. Have you not talked to James?"

Call me crazy, but I assumed they'd have put the pieces together by now.

"Our flights got delayed," Jon says. "I called Lily to feed the cats since I knew you were already gone. Blanka and I only got home this morning."

Oh.

I hear Blanka's voice in the background asking what this is about. "Put me on speaker." A flutter of giddiness moves through me at the prospect of sharing my mushy Valentine story. "You might as well both hear this."

"I'm so confused," Jon says but hits the speaker button anyway as Blanka makes a smart-ass comment about his perpetual state of confusion.

God, I love these two together. Is this where Gabe and I are headed?

"Hi, Gretchen," Blanka says. "Have you gotten a lot done on your dissertation?"

"She's gotten way more than that," Jon says before I can answer. "Who is this Gabe guy? Come on, I want to hear about this dude you've been holed up with in the woods."

"What?" Blanka laughs. "Good for you, Gretchen."

"Thank you." I shouldn't love this so much. But it's the first time in ages I've had a romance worth sharing. I want to draw it out. "So while you were giving me the keys to the cabin and assuring me no one ever uses it, James was doing the same exact thing with his old college buddy."

"Who?" Jon demands. "I know a lot of James's friends, but I don't remember a Gabe."

"Forget the who," Blanka says. "Is this a fling or more?"

"More," I say carefully. "A lot more, I think. I know it's crazy since we just met, but—"

"Not crazy at all," Blanka insists. "There's a lot of interesting science behind attraction. Like this phenomenon known as the Proximity Effect, that refers to how physical and psychological nearness tends to increase interpersonal liking."

"Right, yes." God bless my science geek sister-in-law. "That's it exactly."

"There's also something called the Love Effect," Blanka continues, forever the human encyclopedia. "When you fall for someone, you become immune to his or her flaws. All the negative traits don't matter."

A chilly rush of trepidation moves up my arms, but Jon doesn't let me dwell. "Who, goddamn it? Can we get back to the story, please? Have I met this guy?"

"You have." I bite my lip, hoping this is okay to share. Gabe and I never discussed it, which is dumb in retrospect.

Typical Gretchen. Kiss first, ask questions later.

"Gabe Judson," I say, pushing aside my annoying inner voice. "He and James went to prep school together and also college, but they've kept in touch over the years even though Gabe's in California and—"

"Wait." Jon's voice breaks through like an axe. "You've been trapped in a mountain cabin with Gable Fucking *Judson?*"

Even Blanka gasps. Then a sound like she slugged Jon in the arm. "How did you never mention your family knows the Judsons?" she demands.

There's a buzzing in my ears getting louder and louder. Something's off here. Some piece of the story missing, something no one's telling me.

It takes every ounce of strength not to let my voice shake. "Why do you say it like that?" I ask. "Like he's someone I should know."

"Babe, everyone knows Gable Judson," my brother chides. "Unless they've been living under a rock."

"Or working on a dissertation." There's a sharpness in Blanka's voice that says she's poised to come to my defense. "Not everyone lives life tied to the television."

Not everyone lives life with their head buried in the sand, either, but I'm beginning to think that's what I've done.

Again.

I grip the phone tighter, steeling myself for whatever comes next. Whatever's about to unravel my carefully constructed love story.

"Start at the beginning," I say. "I need to hear this."

My brother takes a deep breath. "Oh, Gretchen."

The kindness in his voice tells me all I need to know. This isn't going to be good, whatever it is.

"There are things you should know about Gable Judson."

* * *

I BARELY REGISTER my trek back to the cabin. My heart thunders like a kettle drum, and my breath is coming in fast, cloudy bursts.

I took off my gloves a mile back because my palms wouldn't stop sweating, and I know all these physiological responses have nothing to do with running four miles on snowshoes.

"He's one of the most legendary directors in Hollywood, Gretchen." The memory of Jon's voice rings in my ears as puffs of crystal white powder spray my face. "Sort of like Quentin Tarantino—"

"Who?"

"Jesus, Gretchen." Jon should patent the big brother sigh. "He doesn't just direct, but also acts in a lot of his movies. How could you not recognize his face?"

Good question. It's one of dozens flying through my mind as the cabin comes into sight, and I brace myself for the confrontation. To demand answers from the man I was dumb enough to think I knew.

I know plenty now. Ten minutes with Google was enough to fill in the gaps. Ten minutes, that's all it took. Why the hell didn't I do that the first night? Why didn't I ask Lily for his last name and spend just a few minutes learning about the guy I'd just kissed?

Because you're an idiot.

Because you didn't want to know.

Because you're the master of burying your head in the sand.

All of that is true and makes me hate myself infinitely more than I could ever hate Gabe.

Tossing my snowshoes on the porch, I clomp through the front door without bothering to kick snow off my boots. I need to see Gabe. I need him to look me in the eye and explain why he lied to me.

He jumps off the couch and starts toward me. "Gretchen, you're back!"

In slow motion, the joy on his face dissolves. He sees my expression and his eyes go blank. His shoulders sag. He freezes mid-step and stares.

"You know." Even his voice is flat.

He stands there looking at me, hands loose at his sides. The look of resignation in his eyes would be enough to break my heart if I weren't so damned mad.

"Gable Judson." My hands clench into fists as I will myself not to cry. "Two-time Academy Award winning director." The words from his IMDb page are burned into my brain. "Actor, producer, and screenwriter with four BAFTA nominations and six Golden Globes. Newest film *Skeleton Dreams* has grossed more than two billion in global revenue and is the reigning box office champion."

"Still?" Gabe sits down hard on the couch like his legs have stopped working. "How—why—"

"How could you not tell me?" I kick the door closed and storm forward, ready for answers. "We talked about our families and careers and childhoods and hopes and fears. Was it all a big joke to you?"

"Gretchen, no." He shakes his head, looking sadder than I've ever seen him. "I didn't want you to know."

Those words, they're the exact ones Alastair said to me.

I didn't want you to know I was still married because you never would have gone out with me.

My breath is coming in fast, shaky pants as I will myself not to cry. "I'm so sick of men deciding for me what I'm allowed to know."

He looks up and I swear I see tears in his eyes. "I'm so sorry," he says. "That first night, I thought you'd google. Or ask James about me or something. When you showed up here, I was sure you already knew."

A fresh wave of shame ripples through me. "Obviously, I should have done my homework." The words are clipped and brittle, not my voice at all. "Obviously, a smarter woman would have."

"That's not what I m—"

"It doesn't matter." I fold my arms over my chest to hide the fact that my hands are trembling. "So you're hiding out, pretending to be someone you're not."

His expression shifts from guilty to guarded. He studies my face a long, long time. "How much do you know?"

"Not nearly enough." And also, way too much. "I know there was controversy about your new film. Critics said it was too violent."

"It *was* too violent. That was the point." He shakes his head and looks down at his hands. "Never mind."

"No, tell me. I want to understand."

"You wouldn't understand," he snaps.

I blink like he's slapped me. Even Gabe looks surprised.

"I didn't mean it like that," he says. "I just meant—since you don't watch movies or—"

"Right, I get it. We're from two different worlds." Until now, I didn't think that mattered.

I stare at him, willing him to say something that will make this okay. That will explain why he's spent the last three days lying to me.

But when he meets my eyes, I know I've lost him. His guard is up. His eyes are hollow. There is no coming back from that.

"The film was meant to provoke," he says. "To start a conversation about violence. About the way we treat each other as a society. Instead—" He shakes his head, a haunted look flashing in those brown eyes.

"I read about the premiere." A wave of sympathy splashes over my anger, cooling it some. "I'm sorry."

He's staring down at his hands again, a million miles away. "They still don't know how he got the gun into the theater. Slipped through the metal detectors or something. I'd just finished my speech when the audience started screaming."

I do my best to picture it, to imagine what that would sound like. Applause mixed with confusion mixed with terror. I watch Gabe's face and wonder if I've ever seen a man more broken.

"You lunged for the gunman." Details online were sparse—I'm guessing for legal reasons—but I do know that. "You tried to get the gun away."

Gabe just shakes his head. "For all the good it did. The bullet hit Wienerman right in the chest. He was killed instantly."

"Wienerman." Why does that sound familiar?

Gabe buries his face in his hands. "My co-director." His voice is like gravel, rough and sharp. "Six-time Oscar winner. The only filmmaker to win the Palme d'Or at Cannes three times. *Rolling Stone* called him the most iconic figure in American film in the eighties and nineties." His voice hitches like the words burn coming out. "Also accused of sexually assaulting more than two dozen actresses over the last four decades."

Oh, Jesus.

"That's how I know the name," I whisper. "It came up at my last girls' night."

Blanka and Bree and Lily raged about career predators. About a fortress of complicit Hollywood bystanders and victims silenced by threats and money and shame. The conversation haunted me for weeks.

I can only imagine what Gabe must feel like being wrapped up in that world.

I try to recall what else I know of the man. "Wasn't he just on trial?"

Gabe nods but doesn't look up. "He skated on a technicality. But there were more cases working their way through the system."

"And—you think he was guilty?"

Gabe pulls his hands from his face, and I'm staggered by the mix of hatred and disgust and gut-wrenching guilt in his eyes. "I fucking *know* he was. Hollywood's full of guys who get away with that shit."

And you chose to work with him?

I don't say this out loud, but he must see it in my eyes.

"I didn't figure out until halfway through filming what a misogynistic prick he was," Gabe says. "The first charges weren't filed until we wrapped."

I nod, not sure what to say. A sick little part of me is glad he's dead. That Gabe's actions changed the trajectory of that bullet.

A bullet meant for Gabe himself.

"You know the worst part?" He shakes his head, and I'm saved from having to guess when he continues. "Actually, *I* don't know the worst part. That I made a film trying to spark change, and it sparked violence? That people died because of *me*? That those women won't get a chance to tell their stories in court?" He takes a shuddery breath. "Or that when the rumors about Wienerman started flying, I fucking *defended* him."

"You couldn't have known—"

"I *should* have known." His words are such an echo of my own that I almost say so, but Gabe's too quick. "I stopped believing him the instant the first victims came forward. The moment things shifted from rumors to accusations, but still. My first instinct was to believe some asshole friend of the family instead of the victims."

There's a lot to unpack there, and I'm not sure where to begin. "But you *do* believe them," I point out. "You said so yourself. And I doubt those women wanted to relive their worst moments in a courtroom packed with cameras. They were spared that indignity, at least."

I'm probably arguing the wrong point, but I can't speak to the film itself. Maybe I'm wrong about the women not wanting closure in court, but that seems right.

It's not for another few seconds that the rest of his words sink in. "Wait, you said *people* died—plural. Who else?"

Gabe shakes his head. "The shooter fled after Wienerman

collapsed. Made it out of the theater and ran right into the path of a vacuum tank truck."

I barely refrain from gasping. "One of those things that suctions out porta-potties?" That definitely wasn't in the articles I read.

"Yeah." Gabe closes his eyes. "He died instantly. That's two deaths on me. Two grieving families. Two sets of lawsuits. And who knows how many more will come? All because I wanted to start a conversation about violence. *Jesus.*"

I step forward, almost afraid to touch him. Gabe's hunched on the couch like a cornered animal, bristling with needles of emotion.

"I'm sorry." I put a hand on his shoulder, heart aching for everyone involved. Gabe. The women. Even the gunman's family. "You could have told me all of that."

He shakes his head slowly, meeting my eyes at last. His glitter with guilt and desperation. "I liked being the guy you thought I was. The humble set builder. An average guy. A man without blood on his hands."

I swallow hard, throat clogging with emotion. "I wouldn't have judged you, Gabe. And I'd never think that."

He looks at my hand on his shoulder like he's not sure what it's doing there. "You would have," he bites out. "I've spent my whole life watching people's faces shift—watching their entire response shift—the second they realize who I am. Gable Judson, son of Hollywood's most powerful family."

"I wouldn't have cared—"

"Yes," he snaps. "You would have."

My anger simmers again. What is it with men telling me how I'm supposed to feel? "I know you're hurting," I say slowly. "But if you take a step back—"

"That's what I did." He shakes his head. "With you, I stepped totally outside myself. You looked at me differently. Like a normal guy. A guy you liked and respected. Is it so wrong that I wanted to pretend for a while?"

And now my anger's boiling again. "You wanted to *pretend*," I repeat. "At my expense."

He shakes his head, burying his face in his hands again. "I'm sorry." The words fall flat, like he's forcing them out.

"Answer me this," I tell him. "And I want you to be honest."

He nods once but doesn't look up. I want to believe that's enough. That he'll tell me the truth this time. "If you could go back to the night we met and be truthful with me from the start, would you?"

His shoulders sag beneath my palm. Five or six seconds pass before he looks up at me. When he does, the pain in those brown eyes hits like a sucker punch.

He doesn't answer. Not right away. I should be glad he's thinking it through, that he's not just hurling another quick lie.

I don't know why the answer matters so much, but it does. People make mistakes, and I can live with that. I can forgive.

But deliberate deception—

"No." Gabe clenches his hands at his sides. "No, I still wouldn't tell you."

The words slam into me with the force of a wrecking ball. "I see."

"I'm an asshole." He closes his eyes, refusing to look at me. Refusing to let me in. "I told you when we met."

"You did." I didn't believe it then. I'm still not sure I do, but it's clear Gabe's convinced.

I take a deep breath. Then another. I need all the strength I can summon.

I take a step back, distancing myself from him. "You can tell yourself these stories about who you think you are—an asshole, a murderer, a liar. And you can tell me stories about the other Gabe—the family man, the brother, the son. But until you figure out which Gabe you are, there's no room in my life for pretenders."

A few more steps back, and I'm almost to the door. Almost to the gear I left scattered like wreckage. Part of me wants him to follow. To come after me and convince me I'm wrong. To ask me to stay.

Instead, he lowers his head into his hands. "I'm sorry," he says into his lap.

"Me, too." I grab my pack and walk away.

CHAPTER 9

GABLE

I let her leave.

Just let her walk out the door like the big fucking coward I am.

"The researchers out at the BONK compound spotted the fox again, so I'm heading out there." She kept stuffing things in her bag, bristling in all-business mode. "The snow's solid, so it won't take me more than ninety minutes to get over there."

"Gretchen, wait—"

"I'll be fine." She stood up and stared at me, daring me to stop her.

I fucking didn't.

"I'll be fine." She repeated it like she was trying to convince herself. Like she wasn't talking about snow conditions or the distance from here to the compound.

It's the distance between Gretchen and me that matters. The distance I let widen to a big, gaping hole the second she walked out the door. What the hell was I thinking?

Not just letting her go but lying in the first place. I know it was wrong; I can admit that. I'm sorry I caused her pain, and I'd take that all away if I could.

But I'm not sorry about the best three days of my whole fucking life. Laughing and loving and sharing pieces of myself with a woman who accepted them with an open heart, exchanging beautiful bits of herself in return. I've never had that before.

I never will again.

She's been gone less than an hour when I stop feeling sorry for myself and start feeling shitty about what I did. *Shittier.* The hurt in her eyes, the betrayal—I put that there.

God, I'm an asshole. I've said it before, but it's never been truer.

For an hour, maybe more, I sit brooding on the front porch. It's below freezing, but I barely feel the cold. I don't feel much of anything except deep, crushing regret.

I should go after her. Screw the snow, I'll just—

The rumble of a truck's engine slaps me from my half-baked plan. I squint through the trees, scanning the space where the road lies buried under two feet of snow. Gretchen. It has to be Gretchen.

I jump from my chair, heart hammering in my chest. She's back. It's my chance to say what I should have told her an hour ago.

I shouldn't have lied.

I wanted you to like me.

I love you so much.

But the truck that rumbles into view has no female occupants. Four men, all big and made bigger by thick parkas and wool hats. There's a huge steel blade on the front of the truck, chewing through the thick crust of snow as it clears a path to the cabin. I squint at the logo on the side, at the words *Ponderosa Luxury Ranch Resort.* That's what kicks my dumb brain into gear.

I step off the porch as the truck grinds to a halt in front of the fallen tree. The passenger door lurches open, and my brother, Dean, steps out.

He stares at me with piercing hazel eyes that have graced the cover of every magazine in America. "Gable." His gaze sweeps me from head to toe, making sure all the pieces are there. "Not what I meant when I told you to get lost."

I'm deciding how to answer when he jumps the fallen tree like a fucking decathlete, striding past the cars and up the walk Gretchen and I shoveled last night.

"Dean." Love for my brother floods out all my other emotions as I grab him in a bro hug that's way too fierce and forceful. "You're here."

I've never been so glad to see my big brother in my whole damn life.

"Dude." He coughs as I crush his ribs. "I just got off a plane. You're going to break a blood clot out of my lungs or something."

Jon's voice slips through our brotherly capsule, oddly jovial. "You look like shit, man." He slides out of the truck with a chainsaw. "Glad you're still standing."

I'm not sure how to take that, but James climbs out after him and surveys the fallen tree. "Quite the mess you've got."

There's the understatement of the century.

As James pulls a second chainsaw from the cab, Mark slings himself out of the driver's seat and reaches into the truck's toolbox for an axe. "Let's get to work."

I start down the steps, ready to do my part. But Dean grabs my arm. "Not you. We need to talk."

"But I want to help." Also, I want to tear shit up. It seems therapeutic.

Mark shakes his head. "Not enough tools."

James surveys the tree, probably doing mathematical calculations. "We'll need your help stacking firewood, but not yet."

Jon starts up the steps, frowning. "Where's Gretchen?"

I try not to stare at the chainsaw in his hand. "Gone. She snowshoed to that old cult compound. I tried to stop her, but—"

"Oh, right." He nods and surveys the tree, seemingly unconcerned his sister just went trudging alone into the snowy woods. "She said she got a call from Fish and Wildlife. They spotted the fox, right?"

"Right." I swallow hard, needing to come clean about what an asshole I've been to his sister. "Look, I—"

"My sister can handle herself." He swings his gaze back to me and flashes a smile with an edge to it. "And she can handle you, too, if you fuck with her."

"Right." I swallow again, not sure what to do with myself.

The other two Bracelyn brothers are swinging into action, arguing about the best way to approach the tree. Mark revs a chainsaw, ending any chance for quiet conversation. As Jon heads off to join them, my own brother grabs me roughly by the arm.

"Come on." Dean nods toward the cabin. "Let's talk."

The urge to unburden myself to someone I shared Legos with is overwhelming. I lead him inside, making a halfhearted offer of coffee.

"No." Dean leans back against the counter and folds his arms over his chest. "Tell me everything."

So I do.

He already knows about the shooting, of course. The lawsuits, too, so I bring him up to speed on the rest. The salmon chowder and the mix-up with the key. The blanket fort and the lies. I leave out the sex stuff, but I'm sure he reads it in my face anyway.

He reads the rest, too. "You love her."

"Yeah." I never said that, but I'm not surprised he guessed. "And I'm a fucking asshole. That pretty much sums it up."

Dean sighs and looks at me like he's not sure whether to hug or punch me. "You're not an asshole."

"You have to say that. You're my brother."

"Your brother is the person best equipped to tell you you're an asshole," he says. "And I'm telling you you're not. Messed up, sure. But not an asshole."

I sink onto the couch and anchor my hands on my knees. "I

wanted her to like me," I admit. "To like me for *me* instead of the Hollywood bullshit. Or to dislike me for me, if that's what it came to. I just wanted to do it without all the baggage."

"You think you can get away from the baggage?" Dean snorts. "That's cute."

"Fuck you." God, I've missed him.

Dean shakes his head and ambles over to sit beside me. I'm not sure he's made up his mind yet about the hugging or the punching, so I edge away just a little.

"You can run a million miles from Hollywood, and it'll always be part of you," he says. "You can change your name, hide under a damn rock, take a vow of silence—it doesn't matter. There's no escaping the way we were raised. Who we are."

"Gee. That's uplifting. Ever consider a career as a motivational speaker?"

Dean elbows me in the ribs. Not hard, but enough to tell me he's not messing around. "A career change may be a good starting point for all of us."

I think about Gretchen and her career quiz and feel shitty all over again. "I fucked up," I tell him. "Really badly."

"Yeah, you did. We all do. It's what you do next that counts."

I shake my head, wishing it were that simple. "Not just with Gretchen, but with everything." I hesitate, not sure I should say the words out loud. "I should never have made that film."

Dean gives me a hard look. "Are you kidding me? *Skeleton Dreams* is your best work."

"It got people killed."

"It got people *talking*," he argues. "They're having the exact conversations you hoped they would about violence and societal norms. You'd know that if you weren't holed up in bumfuck nowhere."

I shake my head, not believing him even a little. "The film will be forgotten by next month. I was naïve to think I could create meaningful change."

My brother stares at me for a long time, like he's weighing whether to tell me something. I brace for the blow. More lawsuits? Another shooting? A scathing spread in *Entertainment Weekly*?

"They announced Oscar nominations yesterday," Dean says quietly. "Did you know that?"

"I—forgot, I guess."

There's a first. Credit goes to Gretchen for making me forget what's normally the most nail-biting day of the year.

"Six nominations," he says roughly. "That's how many *Skeleton Dreams* got. Best director, best screenplay, a bunch of other shit. Don't talk to me about fuckups, Gabe. You've got plenty, but that film isn't one."

I stare at my brother, too stunned to respond.

When his words sink in, I shake my head. "It doesn't change things," I tell him. "Because of me, two men are dead."

"Because of you, a would-be mass murderer shot a serial sex offender before getting himself smashed by a truck filled with shit," he says. "If you can't see the poetic justice in that, maybe you're not the artistic genius everyone thinks you are."

"Maybe not." I'm definitely no genius. No idiot in his right mind would have let Gretchen walk out the door.

That's when I realize I don't care about the Oscar nods. I don't even care about the conversation the film may be sparking, though I'm grateful if that's true.

But none of it matters without Gretchen in my life.

I look my brother square in the eye. "Ever been in love?"

Dean doesn't blink. "Yes."

Right. I know better than to go there.

"It sucks," I tell him. "It makes you feel naked and scared and vulnerable and turned inside out."

"Now who's the motivational speaker?"

I ignore him, needing to get the rest out. "It also makes you feel like Superman. Like there's nothing in the world you can't do, as long as she's part of your world."

Dean frowns. "Can't say it worked out like that for me, but sure." He nods once, eyes still hard. "So what are you going to be? The scared, naked asshole, or Superman?"

Outside, the chainsaws stop whirring. I hear the Bracelyn brothers shouting and glance out to see they've hacked a big void through the tree. The path is clear.

I know what I need to do.

My legs aren't shaking like I think they'll be when I stand up. I start walking, adding steel to my spine as I grab my coat from the peg on the wall.

I turn back to look at my brother. "Superman."

"There you go."

I move toward the door, squaring my shoulders. "I'll be motherfucking Superman."

"Good man," he says. "Wear a cape, it's cold outside."

Dean's laughing as I stride out the door.

CHAPTER 10

GRETCHEN

"*L*et's see if we've got anybody in there." Colleen Mumford creeps slowly through the underbrush, her long braid snagging on a snow-covered branch. Her wife, Patti, sets her free and crawls after her, quiet as a cat.

I tiptoe behind, grateful to be included. They're wildlife biologists intent on collaring the elusive—and nearly endangered—Sierra Red Fox. After four sightings the last two days, we're all hoping the fox they've dubbed Francine has made her way into the live trap.

"Damn." Colleen shoots me an apologetic look. "Darn."

I laugh. "Please. I'm hardly opposed to cursing."

"Well, in that case, fuck me sideways with a blue potato." Colleen sighs. "We've seen Francine at least a dozen times in the last month, but she outsmarts us every time."

"Francine's a smart girl," I acknowledge. "And sneaky."

"We named her for my ex." Patti smiles and checks to be sure the live trap has been reset correctly. "Also smart and sneaky."

I'm not touching that one. "I really appreciate you bringing me out here. What an amazing opportunity."

"Don't mention it." Patti straightens up and nods back toward their cabin. "Come on. Let's get some coffee, and we'll show you those notes we promised."

We trudge back through the snow in silence, our snowshoes making crunchy sounds in the crust of white. It feels good getting back to work, forgetting about Alastair and Gabe and men in general.

All right, I can't forget about Gabe. Can't stop picturing the haunted look in his eyes. Should I have been quicker to forgive?

"In you go." Colleen lines our snowshoes up next to the door and ushers us inside. "Get cozy by the fireplace. I'll bring the coffee and the field notes."

"Thanks." I follow Patti into the living room, admiring the stripped log walls and the rugged beams overhead. "These cabins are great. I never realized the BONK compound was this nice."

Patti laughs as she settles into a cushy gray chair. "They had good taste for a crazy-ass cult."

From the kitchen, Colleen calls out her two cents. "It's been handy getting to stay here. The Feds figured it was a good trade, having us watching over the place."

"It's the perfect home base for research," Patti agrees. "Kind of a shame all the legal crap will be over soon."

"And then what?" I settle onto a brown leather loveseat, leaving the chair next to Patti's for Colleen.

Patti shrugs. "Not sure. Probably someone'll buy the place."

As Colleen and Patti prattle on about the court proceedings for leaders from the Benevolent Order of the New Kingdom, I pick at a speck of chocolate on the knee of my jeans. From Gabe's ice cream? It must be. I keep scratching the spot, conscious of the ache in the center of my chest. I've kept myself busy today but can't ignore the fact that my heart aches like a thumb slammed in a car door. What is Gabe doing?

I'll have to go back eventually to get the rest of my things. If I know my brother, he's already sent a crew to clear the road. Will Gabe be there when I get back?

"So," Patti says softly. "Do you want to talk about it?"

I look up to see her watching me. "Talk about what?"

She smiles and accepts a steaming mug from her wife. "About whatever's got you looking like someone ran over your dog."

"Or your Sierra Red Fox." Colleen hands me a mug of my own and takes a seat beside Patti, eyes filled with sympathy. "It's none of our business, of course. But it sometimes helps talking to strangers."

"Strangers." I scoff and scratch at the chocolate stain again. "I've known you two for half a day and already feel like I've learned more about you than the last two men I've dated."

"Ooof." Patti clucks and shakes her head while Colleen sips her coffee. "From the look of you, I'm guessing this last one meant something."

Something. Everything. God, I've been dumb.

"You could say that," I murmur. "He failed to tell me some pretty major stuff about himself."

The two exchange a look. Something kind and maternal, and my heart floods with sadness. I miss my mother. My father, too.

Mostly, though, I miss Gabe.

Patti blows on her coffee, eyeing me over the rim of the mug. "Well, if it makes you feel any better, we had a rocky start to our relationship."

I grip my mug, grateful to focus on someone else's problems. "How do you mean?"

The two women trade a private smile before Colleen gives a sheepish shrug. "I may have forgotten to mention I was running from the law when we met."

"What? You?" Colleen's about my mother's age, with a salt-and-pepper braid and kind eyes bracketed by laugh lines. She reminds me more of my mom's friends than an ex-con. "What do you mean?"

Colleen sips her coffee and shrugs. "Before I became a wildlife biologist, I might have dabbled in internet hacking."

"Might have?" Patti laughs. "She built a program to hack the computers of guys trolling the dark web for kiddie porn. Once she had evidence, she'd tip off authorities."

"Anonymously." Colleen smiles and settles back in her chair. "The police don't take kindly to hacking."

"Damn." I study Colleen with new respect. "Good for you."

Colleen shrugs, twisting the mug in her hands. "They did arrest a lot of pedophiles, but the authorities weren't amused. Breaking into other people's computers and stealing pictures isn't exactly legal."

Patti pats her wife's knee and smiles. "Anyway, it all worked out in the end."

I suspect there's more to the story than that, but I'm too dumbfounded to know what to ask. "But—" I glance at Patti. "How did you find out?"

She laughs like this is a meet-cute in a romantic comedy. "The police showed up on our fifth date and hauled her away in handcuffs. Until then, I didn't know she even owned a computer."

I shake my head, not sure who I admire more. Colleen for taking down a bunch of pedophiles, or Patti for not fleeing at the words "You have the right to remain silent."

"How did you deal with it?" I ask Patti, glancing quickly at Colleen. "I mean, no offense, but that's a pretty big piece of information to withhold."

"True," Patti admits, lacing her fingers through her wife's. "Sometimes, the ends justify the means."

Colleen sets her coffee down on a coaster and gives me her full attention. "I can give you all the bullshit about how I did it for good reasons. How I wanted to be with Patti and that's the only way I could do it. But you're right, I withheld the truth. I lied, plain and simple."

"And I forgave her." Patti smiles and squeezes her wife's hand. "Plain and simple."

I stare at them. "I'm not sure it's that simple."

"Why not?" Colleen stares me down. "You're the one who gets to decide. Holding on to betrayal is like swallowing poison and waiting for the other person to get sick."

Patti leans out and pats my knee. "It helps to figure out if you're dealing with a serial liar," she says. "Is this someone who fibs about drugs or gambling or sneaking around with other women? Or is it something you can handle?"

Can I handle it? I think about the reasons Gabe lied. Definitely nothing like drugs or gambling. Or other women.

He's nothing like Alastair.

Part of me isn't willing to let this go. "But doesn't that make me a dupe?" I ask. "An idiot who failed to see the signs?"

"Only if you choose to see yourself that way," Patti says. "Or you can see yourself as someone who's forgiving and trusting and willing to see the good in people. Your call."

Damn. What if it's really that simple? If my trusting nature doesn't make me stupid, but hopeful. If my willingness to see the good in people isn't a flaw, but an asset.

And what if Gabe really does love me?

The sound of a truck motor jars me from my thoughts. Patti and Colleen frown, glancing toward the window. "You know anyone with a big white pickup that's got a snow blade on the front?"

"Me?" I stand up and squint out the window. "No, I—"

The words die in my throat as I get a look at the logo.

Ponderosa Luxury Ranch Resort.

"Isn't that the fancy place over near Bend?" Patti stands up and peers out the window as the truck jerks to a stop.

I'm too stunned to answer as the truck doors open and men tumble out like parka-covered logs. My brother's first, cheerful in blue snow pants and wind-chapped cheeks. James is right behind him, almost unrecognizable in a ski cap and black puffy coat. Mark looks the same as always, outfitted in Carhartts and yards of plaid flannel.

And then there's Gabe.

Gabe and a tall guy who looks a lot like him, with dark hair and the same broad jaw.

But I only have eyes for Gabe. His gaze sweeps the cabins, looking for something. *Someone.* The instant his eyes lock with mine through the window, his face changes.

"That must be your man," Patti says.

Beside her, Colleen gasps. "That's not Gable Judson, is it?"

Patti gapes. "Oh my God, it *is.* And *Dean* Judson." She turns and stares at me. "How do you know them?"

"Um...long story?"

There's no time to explain, since Gabe's charging up the walkway. There's determination in his eyes, and something in his stride that sets my heart pounding.

Colleen shoots me a worried look. "Is this okay? Should I send them away or—?"

"No." I shake my head, already moving toward the door. "I want to hear what he has to say."

"You and me both, sister." Patti peers at the line of men trooping up the walkway. "Did he bring a damn army with him?"

"Those are my brothers." I bite my lip as bootsteps get closer. "Well, one's my brother. The others are *my brother's* brothers, plus I guess Gabe's brother and—it's complicated."

Colleen smiles and steps back from the window. "Sounds like my kind of story."

The doorbell rings and the three of us look at each other. "Do you want privacy or want us to stick around and look menacing?" Patti asks.

"Menacing's good." I reach for the door. "He responds well to being held at gunpoint."

I fling the door open before they can ask more questions. There's Gabe on the front steps, looking big and red-cheeked and so handsome my ovaries roll over and twitch.

"Gretchen." He clears his throat. "Holy shit, I'm so sorry."

Well, that's a start.

Patti and Colleen titter behind me, reveling in the unexpected celebrity visit. I hesitate only a second before my heart caves in on itself.

"Come in before you freeze to death." I usher the men inside, mostly to keep from letting all the heat out of the cabin. Mark has to duck to get through the doorframe, and the guy I'm assuming is Gabe's brother is just an inch or two shorter.

Jon and James file in last, looking more than a little bemused. "Ma'am." James nods at the two women. "Sorry to barge in like this. We won't be long."

Patti beams. "Make yourselves at home. Coffee?"

Jon cocks his head. "Um—sure."

I focus my attention on Gabe, not wanting to get distracted. "You said you're sorry. What for?"

He takes a deep breath, squaring his shoulders. "For lying to you. I had plenty of chances to tell you who I was and what I'd done, and I chickened out. I knew how much lying would hurt you, and I did it anyway, and I'm sorry."

I look into those deep brown eyes and take a breath. "I forgive you."

I wait for the rush of lightness Colleen and Patti promised. For the heavy weight to lift off my shoulders. It feels good to say the words, but is this it?

Gabe steps forward, not done yet. "Gretchen, I've never met anyone like you," he says. "You're beautiful and smart and clever and all those things, but you're so much more than that. I love that you name your appliances. I love that you're passionate about fox research, but you have no idea who Seinfeld is. I love that you have a filthy coloring book and an electric ice cream scoop. I love that your instinct is to trust people, even when they're total assholes."

My eyes fill with tears and I blink them back. "You're not an asshole."

The lookalike guy behind him lifts an eyebrow. "Sometimes he is."

"Sometimes we all are," I acknowledge. "I think that's what I'm figuring out. Not that lying's bad and trust is good or that one of us screwed up more than the other. The point is that we're all screwups in some way. And it's up to us to learn from those mistakes so we can be less screwed up the next time."

Colleen and Patti laugh, and I know I should probably introduce everyone. But right now, I'm focused on Gabe. On this wonderful, strong, sensitive, flawed man who's willing to mesh his flaws with mine and make the best of it.

"I'm sorry, too." I reach for his hand, lacing my fingers through his chilled ones. "I'm sorry I left instead of talking it out. And I'm sorry for everything you've been through."

For everything he still has to go through, if the headlines are any indication.

"Thank you." His fingers squeeze mine. "I love you, Gretchen."

"I love you, too."

"Awww." My brother starts to applaud, but James grabs his hand.

"Show some respect."

Mark grunts. "Let 'em kiss."

I'm not sure how I feel about having an audience for that. I'm spared when Colleen clears her throat. "Sorry to interrupt, but I just have to say *Skeleton Dreams* was brilliant. The commentary on violence in our society—I left that theater in tears."

Gabe's hand tenses in mine. Just an infinitesimal amount, but enough to swing my gaze to his. His eyes are warm and shimmering with love, but there's something else.

"Thank you." He stands a little straighter, voice husky with pride and some emotion I can't identify. "That means a lot."

"It's one of the best films I've seen," Patti adds. "If any of you haven't seen it, we're going into town again for the seven-thirty show."

The other men shuffle forward. "I could use a movie night," Mark says. "My wife and daughter are out of town."

Jon shrugs. "Why not?"

The Bracelyn boys introduce themselves to Patti and Colleen, doing their best to explain our complicated family tree. Dean moves to the window, his thoughtful gaze sweeping out over the compound. "There's some definite possibility here."

I don't ask what he means. I don't care, because now I have some privacy with Gabe.

Pulling him aside, I look into his eyes, searching for what's troubling him. "You okay?"

He nods and squeezes my hand. "Yeah. Yeah, I really am. I'll own the fact that I made a lot of mistakes, but maybe *Skeleton Dreams* wasn't one of them."

I grab his other hand, linking us tighter together. "I saw a Google alert about the Oscar nods. Congratulations."

"Thank you." He tightens his grip on my hands. "I might be done making movies, and I'm okay with that. I'm also done hiding. The guy snowed-in with you at the cabin—that's the real me. The Gabe I want to be, and I'm the best version of him when I'm with you. I love you, and I'm committed to being with you no matter what it takes."

And there it is. That rush of feeling I wanted, the certainty that this will all be okay. Emotion floods through me, warm and liquid. "I want the same thing," I murmur. "Wow, that's—that's a big step."

And so distant from my experience with Alastair that they're not even in the same galaxy. That's what I'm realizing, more than anything. I was afraid of trusting Gabe, of getting my heart broken again.

But really, it was my own instincts I had to learn to trust. And right now, they're telling me that Gabe is the real deal.

"I want you to meet my family," he says. "I want to meet yours, and to be by each other's sides for all the good things and the bad. I want long-term, Gretchen."

Tears fill my eyes, and I blink them back. "That sounds good to me." I laugh, a little dumbfounded at how this is unfolding. "Don't you think we should have a date first? Before we start making long-term plans?"

He grins. "What did you have in mind?"

"How about a movie?" I offer. "Your choice."

He laughs and pulls me tight against him. "I'm feeling like a romance, actually."

"Same," I murmur, snuggling into his chest. "Let's go for the happily ever after."

EPILOGUE

GABLE

"Want more popcorn?"

I hold out the container, but Gretchen shakes her head. "I'll get ice cream at intermission."

I laugh and slip an arm around her shoulders. "What makes you think there's an intermission?"

She slips a hand between my thighs, lightly skimming my junk. "It's the upside of banging the guy who owns the drive-in theater."

And the upside of being the only people here besides a scattering of other family members. Jon and his wife, Blanka, are parked about a hundred feet away in a pickup truck piled high with blankets and pillows. They wanted to watch the stars, though from the looks of things, they only have eyes for each other.

"Don't look now," Gretchen whispers, "but I think James's BMW is rocking."

"I'm not looking." I grab another fistful of popcorn, conscious of the fact that we're surrounded by lovebirds.

And I'm grateful to be in their company. Gretchen sweeps a

hand toward the rows of empty cabins just beyond the movie screen. "This is so weird."

"You're going to have to be more specific." I pull her closer, kissing her temple. It's all I can do not to join the ranks of her over-amorous family and invite her into the backseat.

"You guys just up and bought a cult compound," Gretchen says, reminding me we're in the middle of a conversation. "With a drive-in. And a water park. And enough housing to hold—"

"A cult?"

She laughs and shakes her head. "I'm serious. Very weird."

"I prefer the term *interesting*."

"Interesting, then." She sticks a hand in the popcorn bowl, giving in to temptation. "I don't know too many people who'd cough up millions of dollars to buy a vacant cult compound for the sake of a social experiment."

"It's a thoughtfully-planned, self-contained community." I'm reciting the tagline my sisters came up with last week at the family meeting.

Gretchen quirks an eyebrow. "A thoughtfully-planned community of residents who agree to have their lives televised."

"There's that."

In truth, it's a little weird to me, too. And new.

But exciting, too, just like the prospect of moving out here to the middle-of-nowhere Oregon. We all are—Dean, me, Lana, Lauren, Mari, Cooper—plus a whole bunch of strangers who'll be occupying these cabins very soon.

"Did I tell you Dean's narrowed the field for the Chief Financial Officer?" I ask. "He's interviewing her next week. And get this—there's sort of a faint connection to your family."

"My family?"

"Well, your brother's family. The Bracelyns. I think she's a cousin or something."

"Vanessa Vincent?"

"You've met her?"

Gretchen nods and swipes a piece of popcorn. "A couple times. She has a twin sister. I knew she planned to apply."

"That's her." I probably shouldn't say much more about the hiring process, but Human Resources doesn't fall under my umbrella. "Anyway, she's a strong contender to be our new CFO."

Gretchen laughs and grabs another piece of popcorn. "Leave it to your brother to think the financial officer should be hired before medical personnel or law enforcement or schoolteachers."

"Or someone to run an ice cream shop." I grab another handful of popcorn and grin as the opening credits flicker onto the screen. "Here we go. It's time."

"*Finding Nemo* on the big screen." She snuggles closer. "Can I close my eyes through the sad parts?"

I pull her to me, cradling her body against my chest. "I've got you. And there's more happy stuff than sad, trust me."

"I do trust you." She grins and burrows into the space between my arm and my ribs. "So much."

I trust me, too. For the first time in ages.

I trust that making *Skeleton Dreams* wasn't a mistake, just like I trust that walking away from that chapter of my life is the best decision I can make.

I trust that I'll be happy here in Oregon, surrounded by family and friends and the community we plan to build together.

I trust that getting snowed-in with Gretchen is the best damn thing that ever happened to me.

I plant a kiss on the side of her head. "I love you."

"I love you, too."

As Gretchen gives a contented sigh, the screen fills with bright color. It's still no match for what's filling my heart right now. I'm so damn happy I could burst.

The sad scene's approaching, and I lean down to whisper in her ear. "There's a happily ever after. I promise."

She smiles and tips her head up to kiss my chin. "I know there is."

Me, too. I've never been surer of anything.

***

Thank you for reading Gabe and Gretchen's story! This Ponderosa Resort novella was created to kick off a new rom-com series called Juniper Ridge, which features Gabe and his siblings transforming the former cult compound into a tiny town. The result is the sexiest social experiment on television, with a mish-mash of medics, cops, and farmers seeking a fresh start—and maybe a shot at love.

Keep reading for chapter one of *Show Time,* or order it right here:

https://books2read.com/b/47E7q7

And if you're hungry for more Ponderosa Resort rom-coms, the series is complete with book #9, *Dr. Hot Stuff.* Keep reading after the *Show Time* chapter for a sneak peek.

For now, here's the first chapter of *Show Time...*

YOUR EXCLUSIVE SNEAK PEEK AT SHOW TIME

CONFESSIONAL 32.5
Judson, Dean (CEO: Juniper Ridge)

*What? No, of course I'm not fucking camera shy. Jesus, Lauren.
I grew up with the damn things shoved in my face just like you.
Production value? [unintelligible muttering] Can't I just run
the business side of—yeah, I know. All in this together, blah
blah. I still don't see why I have to sit here like a trained
parrot and—[heavy sigh] Fine. But only for the business. It's
not because you're doing the sad little sister face. Or because I
love you.*

Oh, bite me.

* * *

I glance at the clock in my office, trying to decide if I
have enough time to grab coffee. In my old life, I had
an assistant who'd set a hot mug in front of me before I even
thought the word coffee.

But my old life was full of dirty money and blinding lights

and the constant stench of desperation, so getting my own coffee is a small price to pay.

Six minutes. That's how long I have until the candidate for chief financial officer makes her appearance. How long does it take to make coffee, anyway?

"Here are the notes for the police officers' screen tests." My sister, Mari, strides in with a folder in her hands and a pencil speared through her lopsided bun. "Lauren emailed you the video files. I think the psych eval on—"

"Doesn't this seem weird to you?" I fold my hands on my desk as Mari stops moving for once and looks at me. "I mean, we're hiring professionals based on how well they'll perform on camera."

Mari sighs and whacks the folder down in front of me a lot harder than necessary. "We're making a reality show, not staffing the Oval Office. And we're hiring them for specific skills they bring to the community." She gives me the look over the rim of her glasses. "Are we going to keep having this conversation? Because if we are, I'll ask Lauren to tape my response and you can hit play by yourself."

"That sounds about right." Our brother, Gabe, ambles through the door grinning. "I only caught the end of that, but if we're suggesting Dean spends his days in here buffing the banana, we should rethink letting him have the big office."

"Get out." I glance over my brother's shoulder at the clock. "I've got five minutes until my next interview gets here."

"She's already here." Gabe drops into one of my guest chairs, in no hurry to get gone. "That's what I wanted to tell you. She's been out in the waiting room for ten minutes."

Punctual. That's a good sign. I make a mental note as Gabe kicks his legs out and folds his hands behind his head. "She's actually sort of related."

A ripple of unease churns my gut. I'm not a fan of nepotism. I saw way too much of that in Hollywood. "Related to whom?"

"To us," he says. "Well, me. My *wife*." He draws out the word like a guy who has not yet exhausted the novelty of it. To be fair, it's been three weeks since the wedding, and also his wife is awesome. "Gretchen's brother, Jon—his dad has this sister—"

"Jon's *late* father," Mari puts in, always big on establishing the human connection. "Who is no relation to Gretchen because she and Jon had different fathers."

I'm already lost in the branches of my brother's new family tree. "So, we're not talking immediate family here?"

Gabe glares. "Will you let me finish, chief tight-ass?"

I sigh and wave him on, glancing at the clock again. I suppose I'll live without the coffee.

"Anyway, Gretchen's brother's father's sister has these twin daughters, and one of them—"

"Vanessa Vincent," I interrupt. I like how the name sounds rolling off my tongue, strong and no-nonsense. "Harvard MBA, two years with PricewaterhouseCoopers, expertise in forensic accounting, compliance, and internal audit management."

Gabe blinks. "You know all of this?"

"I know everything." Not always, but ever since my personal life took a big nosedive, I've made it my business to foresee all possible landmines. Fool me once and all that.

"Anyway," my brother continues, "she completed our Community Compatibility Questionnaire." He pauses here and smiles at Mari. "Nice job on that, by the way."

My sister nods. "Glad to know the psych doctorate is useful to you," she says dryly.

I give them the universal *hurry up* hand signal, my duty as the eldest brother. "You were saying?"

Gabe swings his focus back to me. "Vanessa's answers in the personal information section were really interesting. Under 'level of interest in finding a spouse or mate,' she chose negative three."

I frown at Mari. "I thought it was a scale of one to ten?"

"It was," she says. "Ms. Vincent somehow found a way to alter the online questionnaire to insert a new answer."

Noteworthy. Noteworthy and...interesting.

"The rest of her responses were the same," Gabe continues. "Under 'I see myself getting married in the next five years,' she went with negative six."

Mari clears her throat. "There's also a write-in answer with that one. It reads, and I quote, 'roughly the same as the odds I will wake tomorrow with an overwhelming urge to drive a flaming fork through my eyeball.'"

"I see." I already liked Ms. Vincent's resumé, but this is giving me a new dimension.

A dimension I relate to on a primal level. The CFO will be my closest working colleague at Juniper Ridge. While a part of this social experiment hinges on participants pairing up, the opposite is vital for me.

"Thank you for the information," I tell them. "I'll take it into consideration."

Gabe glances at his watch and stands up. "Gotta go. Lauren and I are filming B-roll over in the residences."

Mari follows, her bun flopping slightly to one side. "Good luck with the interview," she tells me. "Call us when you're done. I want to go over my proposal for the psych profiles of culinary community members."

"No crazy chefs," I tell her. "Or bakers. Or—"

"Yeah, thanks." Mari rolls her eyes. "Without your input, I'd definitely put psychotic criminals in charge of our food supply."

She's out the door before I can retort, which is just as well. I didn't have anything clever to say anyway. I glance at my watch and see there's no time left for coffee.

Heaving myself out of my chair, I make my way down the hall and into the lobby. For a former cult compound, this place is pretty nice. Case in point, this lodge with its high ceilings and springy cork floors and enough offices for all six Judson offspring. There's also an on-site film studio, which I'll be keeping my distance from as much as possible.

Trudging into the waiting area, I'm struck by its lone occupant. Dark hair with just enough wave to leave it rippling around her shoulders as she taps away on a laptop. Slender curves, which I absolutely shouldn't be noticing. I can't see her eyes until she looks up and hits me square in the chest with the full force of liquid brown irises the color of warm cognac.

She shuts the laptop and shoves it in her bag on the chair beside her, then stands with a bright smile. "Hello."

"Ms. Vincent, I presume?" My voice cracks only a little as I extend a hand and do my best to cover the fact that she's knocked me off balance. "I'm Dean Judson, CEO. Thank you for waiting. Would you like coffee?"

"Absolutely." She shakes my hand with a firm grip. "It's great to finally meet you. My cousin told me so much about you."

"That would be—Jonathan." I met him when I first came to Oregon to rescue my brother from himself. Since Gabe wound up marrying into Jon's family, I can't claim much credit for how great my brother's doing.

"I'm glad you brought that up, actually," I tell Vanessa. "The fact that you're here—it has nothing to do with any family connection. Your credentials were simply impeccable."

"Impeccable, huh?" She grins and slings a gigantic purse over her shoulder in a cross-body style. I keep my eyes locked on her face, unaffected by the sight of the strap pressing a soft path between her breasts.

"Impeccable," I repeat. "Former accounting manager for America's second-largest television network. Treasurer and CFO for a Silicon Valley startup." I take a step back, intent on keeping a professional distance between us. "In your last role, you raised more than $50 million in venture capital for a company devoted to establishing sustainable farming practices in third-world countries."

Vanessa gives a low whistle. "You did your homework. Some of that wasn't even on my resumé."

"I believe in being thorough." There's an understatement. "Come on. Coffeemaker's this way."

I lead her into the breakroom, hoping like hell one of my siblings was kind enough to brew some.

No dice. Lana didn't even wash her mug that says, *"I'm actually not funny. I'm just mean and people think I'm joking."*

I rinse it and set it in the drying rack before rummaging in the back of a lower cupboard for my favorite mug. I've had it twelve years and keep it tucked away so it doesn't end up lost or broken or nabbed by one of my five siblings. Turning to face the coffeemaker, I assess the task at hand. Christ, this thing has more buttons than my HP 12C Platinum accounting calculator.

But if I can mastermind a decade of Hollywood's biggest real estate deals and filmmaker financing, I can make a simple cup of coffee. I punch a few levers and yank at something that spurts a sharp hiss of steam. Finally locating the part that holds coffee grounds, I dump the soggy ones in the trash and hunt for a new filter.

"Did you have any trouble finding the place?" I ask.

"Not at all." Vanessa leans back against the counter to watch me work. "The directions you sent were spot on. This is definitely in the middle of nowhere."

"That's by design, I suppose."

"No joke," she says. "The BONK founders wanted their privacy."

One of the few things to admire about the former members of the Benevolent Order of the New Kingdom, the former cult that built this place.

I stare into the vessel where the coffee grounds go. How much do I put in here? I could check the filter I just tossed, but it seems in poor taste to paw through the trash with a prospective job candidate watching. And she *is* watching; I can feel her eyes on me.

"Need help?" she asks cheerfully. "I've got some pour-over coffee packs in my purse. Sugar and creamer, too."

"Nope, I've got it." Noteworthy about the coffee, though. Well-prepared accountants are a plus.

Dragging a flowered tin from the back of the cupboard, I pry off the lid. Coffee grounds. I settle for eyeballing it, dumping in a hefty pile into the fresh filter before slamming the trap door shut. Now where does the water go?

Glancing at Vanessa, I decide to get the interview started. "I assume you've been briefed on the concept of *Fresh Start at Juniper Ridge.*"

I cross my fingers she hasn't caught on that I don't know what the hell I'm doing. Not with the coffee, anyway. I've got a handle on the rest.

"Of course," she says. "Reality television show centered around a thoughtfully planned, self-contained community." She's reciting straight from our website, and I admire that. I admire it a lot. "You're bringing in a diverse group of individuals representing a variety of professions, backgrounds, and lifestyles, and setting the stage for them to create a completely sustainable microcosm of society."

"Correct." Seriously, where does the water go? I yank at a lever and end up unplugging the machine. "It's part social experiment, part entertainment, part a chance to resurrect a piece of property with some questionable history."

"BONK was certainly one of the more—*colorful* cults."

I appreciate that she's being tactful, but it's not necessary. "You mean the part where they believed their leader was the progeny of an extraterrestrial prophet and Charlie Sheen, or the part where they touted mass orgies as a means of growing the roster?"

She laughs. "All of it. I take it you won't be shying away from that history?"

"Might as well let viewers learn from others' missteps so they're not doomed to repeat them."

From the corner of my eye, I see her stiffen. When I look up, she's dropped her shoulders again. Or maybe I imagined the whole thing.

Turning back to the coffeemaker, I pry off a piece that turns out to be the water chamber. Now we're getting somewhere.

"The BONK founders created one hell of an impressive town, so we're just giving it new legs." Belatedly, I realize I've just cursed at a job candidate. But if cursing offends her, she's unlikely to fit the Juniper Ridge family. Maybe it's a job test.

Or maybe she's the one testing me, waiting to see how badly I'll screw up the coffee thing before I ask for help. I can't tell from her face if she's judging. Her expression's impassive, patient, even serene.

Damn, she's beautiful.

If I weren't dead inside, I might notice things like that.

"It's a clever concept," Vanessa says, jarring me back to the fact that we're in job interview mode, even though we haven't made it to my office. "And financially speaking, there's high potential for revenue. The files you sent on advertisers who've committed—I took the liberty of setting up some spreadsheets, which I'd be happy to show you."

"That—that would be great." I glance at her, braced for the coquettish smile I've gotten from dozens of social climbing show biz types. The *'show me your private office,'* or *'Let me prove how much I want this job.'*

But Vanessa's slipping a pair of glasses out of her purse and setting up her laptop on the breakroom table. As the coffee starts to perk, she opens up Excel and dives right into the numbers.

"In this table here, I've factored in the living costs for each member of the cast." She glances up and lifts a brow. "Are you calling them cast members or residents or what?"

"Community members." A little dumbfounded, I drop into the seat beside her. "You already started running numbers?"

"I emailed the hiring manger to request some data—Marilyn?"

"Mari." Who, of course, failed to mention this. "Go on."

"Anyway, this takes into account the economic contributions of each community member—for instance, farmers, chefs, grocers—everyone who represents the food supply is shown in this column, while those who contribute to safety—police and fire, for example—are represented here on the grid."

I listen to her rattle off numbers, staggered by how much she's put into this. We had two other candidates make it to this round, and neither took it this far. I listen with rapt attention, impressed she's thought of aspects of this that my five siblings and I hadn't considered in months of planning.

"I'd be happy to email this to you if you'd like a closer look." She smiles and glances at the coffeemaker. "Smells like that's ready. Want me to get it?"

"Definitely not." I jump up like my chair's on fire and hurry to grab mugs. "If we were to offer you the CFO position, I'd want to be clear you're not my assistant. You and I would be partners on the business side of this operation."

She nods and tucks a shock of hair behind one ear. "And your siblings—they're mostly on the production side?" She accepts the mug I hand her, wrapping her fingers around the warm ceramic instead of grabbing the handle. "I find the whole dynamic fascinating."

"Yeah, Gabe's directing, working with our sister, Lauren. She's the producer." I blow on my coffee, conscious of an odd sting in my nostrils. "There's also Mari—Marilyn—she's a psychologist. The social component was her brainchild."

"And Lana." Vanessa twists the mug in her hands but doesn't take a sip. "Public relations, right?"

"Yep, and then Cooper. An actor, though he'll be taking a different role with this endeavor."

I wait for her to ask about Coop. Most people pry for gossip about the Judson family hellraiser, but Vanessa doesn't go there.

"You have a lot of talent in one family." She lifts her mug in a mock toast, then raises it to her lips.

The instant she sips, her brown eyes bulge. "Holy shit!" She sputters into the mug, spraying coffee as she jumps from her chair. "Did you brew napalm?"

I take a sip from my own mug and choke. "My God. It's like battery acid."

She's wiping her tongue with a paper towel, gagging as she does it. "I thought you went heavy on the grounds, but this is like drinking tar."

Handing me the roll of paper towels, she bends to rinse her mouth in the sink. Swishing and spitting, she coughs as she edges sideways to make room for me.

"Sorry," I mutter, scraping my tongue with my teeth. "It's—uh —my first time making coffee."

"I kinda guessed by watching you," she says. "But this is beyond awful."

I finish gulping water from the tap and stand to face her. Water dribbles down my chin, and this is so far from the interview I imagined that there's no point in saving it. "You knew I was screwing it up, but you didn't say so?"

She folds her arms over her chest and stares me down. "It's not my style to micromanage. I was giving you the benefit of the doubt that you had a different way of doing things."

"And that I wasn't trying to kill you?" I shake my head, feeling like an asshole. "I really am sorry."

"Don't mention it. What kind of coffee is that, anyway?"

I open the cupboard and pull out the flowery tin. "Jovan's Special Blend," I read off the label.

"Jovan?" She frowns. "The cult leader? Weren't they raided like two years ago?"

I sniff the contents of the canister. "What does tear gas smell like?"

Vanessa grimaces and dumps the contents of her mug down the sink. "I think I'll skip the coffee, thanks."

"Good thinking." I start to chuck the whole canister, then stop. "Maybe I should have this tested."

She sniffs the contents and shrugs. "It smells like coffee. Really bad, really old coffee, but still coffee."

I smell it myself, and she's right. So maybe it's a case of user error.

"Come on." I put the lid back on and set the canister on the counter. "There's a coffee shop on the other side of the compound. It's not fully operational yet, but at least the coffee is drinkable."

Vanessa cocks her head. "Does this mean we're continuing the interview?"

She's already hired as far as I'm concerned, but yeah. I should do my due diligence. Failing to do that has burned me before, and no way am I repeating that.

A chill snakes down my arms, and I wonder if she feels it. The way she's looking at me is so intense, so intimate, that it stalls the breath in my lungs.

Vanessa takes a step back. "I should tell you up front that I'm here for a fresh start," she says. "I've had bad luck in the past mixing business and—and—*not* business, so this role would be purely professional for me."

I stare at her as my subconscious jumps up and down yelling.

You're hired. You're so fucking hired.

But I've learned not to listen to that asshole.

Clearing my throat, I turn toward the door. "Let's get that coffee."

***

139

Want to read more? Get your hands on *Show Time right* here:
Show Time
https://books2read.com/b/47E7q7
If you're ready to keep rolling with the Ponderosa Resort series, keep reading for a glimpse at *Dr. Hot Stuff*. Full disclosure: This story kicks off with some big spoilers from the rest of the series, so if you don't already know who was hiding in James Bracelyn's guest room in *Stiff Suit* or what Mark Bracelyn learns about his DNA in *Hottie Lumberjack*, you might want to stop here.

Otherwise, here's your preview of *Dr. Hot Stuff...*

YOUR EXCLUSIVE SNEAK PEEK AT DR. HOT STUFF

ISABELLA

"*T*hank you all for being here."

James adjusts his tie, then starts a slow circuit around the conference room. He picks up a lamp and studies the underside. Frowning, he puts it back and moves on to the stapler. I wait for one of my other siblings to address this peculiar behavior.

I don't wait long.

"For fuck's sake, give it a rest." Mark sounds gruff, but I saw him rescue an injured duck by the pond yesterday. I know what sort of man he is.

"Seriously, bro." Jonathan folds his arms over his chest and regards our older brother with bemusement. "No one bugged the damn conference room."

James looks utterly unconvinced, but before he can object, Bree stands and touches his arm. "Would you feel safer having this meeting somewhere else? Your cabin or maybe the resort stables?"

My brother's eyes drop to the baby strapped to Bree's chest in an odd American contraption called a Cuddlebug. It's a bit like the slings they use in my home country, though in Dovlano they're made of silk instead of cotton. I'm certain my mother never wore one, but perhaps my nanny did.

The sight of his nephew must soften something in James because his green eyes warm just a little. "I'm being cautious," he says. "Switching meeting venues won't be necessary."

Across the table, Sean raps a long-handled spoon on the table. "We'd have plenty of privacy in the walk-in cooler. Just need our winter coats and—"

"Is there a reason you brought a damn spoon to this meeting?" Jonathan reaches over to grab it, but Sean snatches it back.

"Maybe I felt like stirring up shit?" Sean grins and turns his attention back to James. "Or maybe it's for the guest in cabin 34. I'm running it over right after this."

Mark frowns. "Someone requested a special fucking spoon?"

"I guess he's making stew or something." Sean shrugs. "Beats me, but I've got enough spoons. I can share."

Bree lifts one perfect eyebrow. "Is he aware he doesn't need to prepare his own meals? We do have a Michelin starred chef on the premises."

"Yeah, but he sucks." Jon laughs and makes another grab for the spoon, and Sean retaliates by whacking him on the arm with it.

"Keep that up, and I'll bring lima beans and clam pizza for poker night." Sean tucks the spoon safely in the pocket of his chef's coat. "No homemade pretzels and beer cheese dip for you."

Mark grumbles something profane while James launches into a lecture on professional meeting conduct. While the Bracelyn men are squabbling, Bree leans toward me with a sly little smile.

"Don't worry," she whispers. "He already made the pretzels and saved extra cheese for us since ladies aren't invited to poker night."

"How lovely." I'm not sure I've ever had beer cheese sauce, but I appreciate being included. "Who goes to poker night?"

I know full well it's all the Bracelyn brothers, plus a few men in the community. There's something quite specific I'm wondering, but I don't have the courage to ask.

Will Bradley Parker be there?

Bree smiles like I've spoken aloud. "These dorks started the poker night thing." She gestures at our brothers, who are still busy bickering. "Austin joins when he's not on duty. Oh, and Bradley Parker, of course. You remember Dr. Parker?"

Heat floods my cheeks, and I pray she doesn't notice. "Of course. Nice man. Very polite."

It's an idiotic thing to say, but Bree only smiles. "It's probably the military background."

"Military?"

She shrugs like it's unimportant, but this is an enormous nugget of information for my collection of personal data on the handsome doctor. "He started as an Army doc, but got out when his father died," Bree says. "So he could be there for his mom."

"I see." I had no idea about any of this, though we've crossed paths plenty in the year I've spent at Ponderosa Resort.

Bree's watching me closely, and I swear she reads my thoughts. "He's single, by the way."

My cheeks get even hotter, but before I can respond, James claps his hands to bring the meeting under control.

"Welcome, Isabella," he says. "I know this is your first official meeting as part of the Ponderosa Resort team, and we're happy to have you with us."

A murmur of agreement rolls around the table, filling my chest with sunshine. I'm thrilled to be included, even if I'm unsure how best to contribute.

"Shall I take notes?" I pluck a pen from a polished metal container and scan my siblings' faces. "I'd like to do my part."

"No notes." James frowns at the pen until I lay it down and fold my hands. "No record of this conversation should leave this room."

Oh.

Now he's got my attention. Everyone else's, from the looks of things, though no one appears as alarmed as I'm feeling now. Do they know something? Have they heard from my mother?

Or worse, from the Duke of Dovlano, the man who raised me as his own until I learned my biological father was a man named Cort Bracelyn. That's what brought me here, much to the chagrin of the Duke and Duchess.

I realize I'm fidgeting with the notepad, so I push it away and hide my hands under the table. "Right. Of course, strictly confidential."

Jonathan gives a hearty laugh. "Watch out, Iz," he says, delighting me with the casual nickname I've acquired only recently. "You write anything down, he'll make you tear it up and eat the pieces."

"I've got a great recipe for that." Sean pushes up the sleeves of his chef's coat and leans back in his chair. "A little heavy cream, a touch of tarragon, and then—"

"Will you please be quiet?" James is scowling as he takes his seat. As the CEO, he's the one running this meeting. Or maybe it's because he's the eldest brother. I'm still not entirely familiar with this country's customs, let alone Bracelyn traditions.

James glances at me, and his expression softens again. "We're very glad you're with us, Isabella. You're part of this family, and as we've all stated before, you are welcome to stay with us for as long as you like."

I nod as my brain telegraphs words I won't say aloud.

How's forever?

I don't say this aloud. It's an impossibility, of course. I simply fold my hands on the table and nod like the perfect lady I was raised to be. "Thank you," I tell him. "All of you have been so gracious since my arrival."

Gracious doesn't begin to cover the fact that Jonathan gave me an actual kidney mere days after I landed in Oregon. It's been almost a year, and even though I've thanked him daily, I should probably do so again.

Before I get the words out, James resumes his speech. "Typically in these meetings, we go around the table and assess what's happening with resort operations," he says. "We review financials, discuss future plans, consider any requests we might have for major events or guests with special needs."

Jon snorts at that. "Like the guy who visits a luxury resort to make stew?" He nods at the spoon in Sean's pocket. "That's the big bald guy, right? The one in cabin 34?"

"Creepy motherfucker." Mark frowns. "Checked in yesterday, and I'm pretty sure he's packing heat."

"Heat?" I'm not familiar with the term.

"A gun." Bree glares at our brothers. "Don't scare her like that. No one shows up armed to stay at a luxury resort."

A shiver ripples up my arms. I know who they're talking about now. I spotted him across the lawn this morning and tried to convince myself it wasn't him. It couldn't be, right?

But I know I wasn't seeing things, just like I know I can't breathe a word to my siblings about their new resort guest. Not yet, anyway.

"Would anyone like tea?" I start to stand, desperate to be helpful. "I'm happy to go fetch some."

Bree gives me an odd look. "I think we're okay, but if you'd like something, I can ring for someone to bring it."

"No, no—I'm fine." I sit back down, resigned to feeling like a burden. An interruption in the family dynamic. "Go on, please. I don't want to hold up the meeting."

James pauses a moment, then looks me in the eye. "Isabella, there are a few things you should know about this family." Another pause, this one longer than the first. "A few...shall we say, *sensitive* items for discussion."

Mark grunts. "Understatement of the fucking century."

James regards him with a look I can't read. "Would you like to address the first item on the agenda?"

Mark shrugs and scrubs a hand over his beard. "I'm a bastard." He announces this like he's just told us he prefers honey ham over prosciutto, then continues. "I mean, yeah, my mom never married Cort Bracelyn, but he paid a fuck-ton in child support, even though he knew damn well it wasn't his batter in the oven."

"Beautifully put." Sean's smile is a whole lot softer than Mark's voice. "I mean, we're all bastards in one way or another, so—"

"Can we please stop with the bastard talk?" Bree bounces the baby in his little holder and gives me a cheerful smile that doesn't cancel out the tiredness in her eyes. "Biology doesn't matter in this family. Even though we didn't know about you until last year, we love you the same as anyone else."

"Thank you." Tears spring up, but I blink them back. "I love you, too. You've been so kind and generous and wonderful, and I can't believe how warmly you've all welcomed me."

It surely must have shocked them learning their father sired a secret baby with a Southern European duchess, and I can't say I wasn't startled to learn I had five half-siblings in America, all with different mothers. Our father produced offspring far and wide, and I wish sometimes I'd met him.

"That brings me to my next point." James takes a deep breath. "The following information cannot leave this room. Understood?"

I nod slowly, nerves prickling the hairs on my arms. "Of course."

"James." Bree glowers again. "Stop scaring her."

He gives a beleaguered sigh. "There's something you should know about our father. Something…not exactly legal."

"Or ethical," Sean adds.

"Or moral," Jonathan puts in.

Mark snorts. "This should go on his goddamn tombstone."

I swivel my gaze back to James, breathing deeply to mask my nervous energy. There's a twinge deep in my low abdomen where the doctors transplanted my new kidney, and I swear I feel a faint tug. "What is it?"

James flattens his palms on the table and looks me dead in the eye. "Our father is alive."

I blink. "I beg your pardon?"

Sean gives a choked laugh. "You're a helluva lot politer than the rest of us when we found out."

My brain is reeling, trying to compute what he's just told me. "But—I saw the obituary. The funeral, parts of it were televised."

James scowls. "Our father appreciated flashy things."

"That's putting it mildly." Bree strokes the baby's fuzzy head. "I once watched him spend ninety thousand dollars on diamond-studded cowboy boots."

I survey their faces, confirming this isn't some practical joke. "Where is he?"

Jonathan shrugs. "No one knows. He's been laying low since he faked his own death."

My gaze lands on James again, since he's running this meeting. He's also grinding his teeth to powder if the clenching of his jaw is any indication. "There was an *incident* several years ago," he says slowly. "He promised to keep his distance, as his presence would obviously cause quite a disturbance at this point."

There's a pounding in my head, and it's only partly from this news they've shared. They've opened up Pandora's Box, and I can't imagine what might leap from it next. "Wow," I breathe, at a loss for words. "What a secret."

My head spins wildly, threatening to roll right off my shoulders. I tuck my hands beneath my thighs so no one sees them shaking. Can they tell I'm feeling anxious? All this talk of secrets has me jumpy and paranoid.

I take a steadying breath, reminding myself to stay calm. They don't know; they can't possibly know.

But the way they're watching me leaves my mouth dry and my vision a bit blurry. I think I might faint.

"Isabella?" Bree touches my arm. "Are you okay?"

I nod because I'm not sure I can find words. It's not just the news that shocked me. It's the knowledge that these people—this family I've known mere months—they've entrusted me with their deepest, most safeguarded secret.

Meanwhile, I sit here like a deceitful, lying, horrible excuse for a—

"Does he contact you?" I blurt the question without thinking it through, needing to say something so they stop staring. "I mean, are you still in touch?"

"No." James presses his lips together. "Not at this time."

I'm certain there's more to this story, but I don't want to pry. It's enough that they're bringing me into the fold. That they're sharing something this monumental with the sister who barely counts as a family member.

I shiver, then do my best to mask it as a sassy little shimmy. Not the most appropriate response under the circumstances, but perhaps they'll mistake it for a seizure. That may be preferable. Can I fake a medical episode and duck into the restroom? I just need a few moments to collect myself, to get my nerves back in order.

"Hey." Jon's voice is achingly kind, and the tears prick my eyes again. "It's a lot to take in, I know. We all kinda freaked out on James when we learned about this, so don't feel bad if you're reeling right now."

"Thank you." I grab a tissue from the center of the table and dab at my eyes, even though I've done well keeping my tears in check. It's mostly just a ruse, an attempt to hide the terror I'm sure must show on my face. "I appreciate you sharing this with me. I promise I'm good at keeping secrets."

This is the truest, most honest thing I've said since this meeting began.

I swallow hard, forcing myself to make eye contact with each sibling. James, Sean, Jonathan, Mark, Bree. One by one, I pray they can't see the panic in my eyes.

That they'll never learn how much I've misled them.

Or how quickly time is running out.

***

WANT TO KEEP READING? Grab *Dr. Hot Stuff* right here: https://books2read.com/u/3G2VKa

DON'T MISS OUT!

Want access to exclusive excerpts, behind-the-scenes stories about my books, cover reveals, and prize giveaways? You'll not only get all that by subscribing to my newsletter, I'll even throw you a **FREE** short story featuring a swoon-worthy marriage proposal for Sean and Amber from *Chef Sugarlips*.

Get it right here.

http://tawnafenske.com/subscribe/

ACKNOWLEDGMENTS

Huge thanks to Fenske's Frisky Posse for the speedy reads and fab reviews. You ladies are the best! I'm especially grateful to Regina, Jen, and Adrienne for catching those pesky last-minute typos.

Thank you to Linda Grimes for being an awesome critique partner and all around wonderful human.

I'm endlessly grateful to agent Michelle Wolfson for being my partner in crime these past 10+ years.

Much love and thanks to Wonder Assistant Meah Meow for striving to keep me organized and slightly sane (ha!).

I'd be a hot mess without Susan Bischoff and Lauralynn Elliott of The Forge for the amazing editorial work, so THANK YOU. Thanks also to Lori Jackson Design for the fantastic teaser graphics.

Love and gratitude to my family, Aaron "Russ" Fenske and Carlie Fenske (and Paxton!) and to Dixie and David Fenske for always being there. Thanks also to Cedar and Violet for being kickass kids who make me grateful I won the stepmom lottery.

And thanks especially to Craig for your infectious laugh, your sexy hands, and your amazing heart. Love you, hottie.

ABOUT THE AUTHOR

When Tawna Fenske finished her English lit degree at 22, she celebrated by filling a giant trash bag full of romance novels and dragging it everywhere until she'd read them all. Now she's a RITA Award finalist, *USA Today* bestselling author who writes humorous fiction, risqué romance, and heartwarming love stories with a quirky twist. *Publishers Weekly* has praised Tawna's offbeat romances with multiple starred reviews and noted, "There's something wonderfully relaxing about being immersed in a story filled with over-the-top characters in undeniably relatable situations. Heartache and humor go hand in hand."

Tawna lives in Bend, Oregon, with her husband, step-kids, and a menagerie of ill-behaved pets. She loves hiking, snowshoeing, standup paddleboarding, and inventing excuses to sip wine on her back porch. She can peel a banana with her toes and loses an average of twenty pairs of eyeglasses per year. To find out more about Tawna and her books, visit www.tawnafenske.com.

f **y**

At the Heart of It

This Time Around

Now That It's You

Let it Breathe

About That Fling

Frisky Business

Believe It or Not

Making Waves

The Front and Center Series

Marine for Hire

Fiancée for Hire

Best Man for Hire

Protector for Hire

The First Impressions Series

The Fix Up

The Hang Up

The Hook Up

The List Series

The List

The Test

The Last

Standalone novellas and other wacky stuff

Going Up (novella)

Eat, Play, Lust (novella)

Made in the USA
Middletown, DE
25 February 2022